Their Bond Through Jade

Iris Blobel

THEIR BOND THROUGH JADE
Copyright © 2017 IRIS BLOBEL
All rights reserved.
www.irisblobel.com

This is a work of fiction. Names, places, characters, and events are fictitious in every regard. Any similarities to actual events and persons, living or dead, are purely coincidental. Any trademarks, service marks, product names, or named features are assumed to be the property of their respective owners, and are used only for reference. There is no implied endorsement if any of these terms are used.

All rights reserved. No part of this publication may be reproduced, distributed, or transmitted in any form or by any means, including photocopying, recording, or other electronic or mechanical methods, without the prior written permission of the author, except in the case of brief quotations embodied in a review and certain non-commercial uses permitted by copyright law.

"Like karma, destiny is neither good nor bad, it just is."
—Dorothy Holder

Other Titles by Iris Blobel

ALINTA BAY SERIES:
DEFYING RULES
TELL IT TO MY HEART
BETWEEN GOODBYE AND HELLO
TOUCH ME

NEW ZEALAND SERIES
THEIR BOND THROUGH JADE
IN THE SHADOWS OF A LIE

FERMOSA BAY SERIES:
ECHOES OF THE PAST
BIGALOW

BEGINNINGS SERIES:
NEW BEGINNINGS
MORE BEGINNINGS
FRESH BEGINNINGS
LITTLE BEGINNINGS

STANDALONE BOOKS:
JOURNEY TO HER DREAMS
SWEET DREAMS, MISS ENGLAND
INNOCENT TEARS

One

WHEN Tiffany Cahill opened the door and laid eyes on the police officers, memories flooded back of the horrid day the year before when she'd been dragged to the police station. Everything inside her tensed as she checked the lever for the screen door to make sure it was locked. She rubbed her damp palms against her pants.

"Miss Cahill?" the male police officer asked, his dark brown eyes focussing on her.

Scared, she wasn't able to find her voice, she bit her lip and simply nodded.

"Miss Tiffany Cahill?" the female, and younger, officer asked.

Tiffany nodded again. If she focussed on the officer's flaming red hair beneath her cap, she wouldn't have to meet her eyes. But she allowed herself a cautious peek at the officers' faces.

Their expressions were unreadable, which was worrying.

"I'm Senior Constable Jones. This is Sergeant Harris." The officer paused for a moment. "We would like to ask you a couple of questions in regard to Thomas Terrill."

"Who?" Tiffany asked, hardly above a whisper. Her whole body shook, and she knew she had to sit down soon or she'd faint.

"Thomas Terrill," Jones repeated. "He was up on charges last year for the possession of drugs. The file states you were involved—"

"There's no way I'll come with you." Her voice was louder than intended, panic rising within her. "You can't make me—"

"Miss Cahill," Jones said with a calm voice.

"We're not here to take you with us, but to ask you a few questions," Sergeant Harris explained, pulling out a little notepad from his shirt pocket, opening it with an expert snap. "Is there anybody with you at home?"

Tiffany frowned as she shook her head. Anxiety raced through the pit of her stomach, and she had to resist the urge to step back to shut the door.

"Anybody you can call?"

His voice was soothing, and when Tiffany met his eyes through the screen door, she noticed something that conveyed trust. And there was a need inside her to trust him, yet every fibre in her told her to not open the door. Never again would she let the police take her to the station and treat her like a criminal.

She bit her lip again, desperate to figure out whom to call, when she replied, "My brother."

Harris nodded. "Thomas Terrill was charged with possession of drugs last year. You are noted as a witness." He paused, checked his little notepad, and continued, "He's also known as Hudson Ford."

Leaning her head against the door, Tiffany took a deep breath to steady herself.

"Are you okay, Miss Cahill?" Harris asked.

"Please open the door," Jones requested.

Holding up her hand, Tiffany replied, "I haven't seen him since last year. I have nothing to do with whatever trouble he's in." Her entire body trembled, anxiety rushing through her like a tidal wave. She took another two deep breaths before standing straight to meet Harris' gaze.

He searched her eyes before he assented with a nod and held out a business card. "We need to talk to you. I can assure you you're not in trouble, but we need your help." He squeezed the card into the small gap of the doorframe. "This is my number. Please call in when you have somebody with you, and we can have a talk."

She nodded, appreciating him leaving the card in the door and not insisting on opening up.

"Will you be okay, Miss Cahill?" This time Jones asked.

The simple answer was no, but again, she nodded, hoping for this nightmare to end soon.

Senior Constable Jones and Sergeant Harris left, and Tiffany watched them drive off in their car. Only then did she close the door, leaning against it, and then slowly sliding down. Clasping her legs against her chest, she laid her head on her knees and took a few deep breaths until her heart rate returned to normal.

Tiffany wasn't sure how long she sat there before she was finally able to get up and reach the phone in the kitchen. She stared at the modern cooking area in front of her as if she was seeing it for the first time. The old wooden cupboards contrasted with her fancy new fridge and oven. The window more or less right in front of her with the view to her neglected back yard. She stepped to the wooden table near the wall and sat before dialling the familiar number. It didn't take long for someone to answer.

"Hello?" came an unfamiliar man's voice.

Tiffany hesitated, but hung up without giving it a second thought. Checking the numbers by pushing *redial*, she pressed *connect* when she was sure. With her heartbeat up a notch, she focussed.

"Hello?" the same man answered, this time with irritation.

Frayed with confusion, she moved her mouth soundlessly until she got her bearings, "Uhm, can I talk to Steve, please?"

"He's not home."

"Who…who are you?"

"My name is Mat. Can I leave him a message?"

Running a hand through her short hair, she racked her brain to put one and one together. This person definitely had a little Kiwi accent. But who the hell was he?

His next question hauled her back to their conversation. "Are you okay?"

"Of course I am. Please let him know I called," she snapped, still out of sorts, and hung up, never giving him a chance to reply.

Breathing hard, she tried to calm herself and reduce the adrenaline that had shot through her and left her shaking all over. She took another deep breath before she walked to the sink to rinse her clammy hands and make a cup of tea. The sound of the phone made her jump, and she rushed back to grab it, nearly knocking over the vase of flowers, cursing the police all the way as well as Hudson, the bastard, who had left her in hospital bruised and beaten up last year.

"Steve?"

"It's Mat. How about you tell me your name so I can ask Steve to return your call?"

"How did you get my number?"

"I hit the redial button," he replied, as if surprised by her question.

A smile twitched at Tiffany's lips. He knew how to help himself. And he cared. "It's Tiffany. My name is Tiffany."

"Nice meeting you, Tiffany, even though it's over the phone. So, you're sure you're okay?"

Tiffany hesitated, but noticed how talking to him calmed her. A quietness inside her began to push away the troubling fears, helping her to relax. "Who are you?"

"My name's Mat, but I've already told you that."

There was no malice in his voice. She sat on one of the chairs, her body relaxing bit by bit. "Steve never mentioned someone called Mat."

He laughed. "You know all his secrets?"

"No. But, considering I'm his best friend, I believe, he would have mentioned a friend staying with him."

"Let me think, I can't recall him mentioning your name, either."

His voice had a teasing tone, and Tiffany was starting to like him. It was exactly what she needed after opening the door to the police.

"After his girlfriend, I'm the next most important person in Steve's life," she said, trying hard to match his humour. "And there's never been a mention of a person named Mat. I'm pretty certain of that."

"Damn that little bugger. Here I thought we were best buddies." He paused for a second then added, "Tell me, Tiffany, why were you so upset?"

"You tell me first how Steve knows someone from New Zealand."

He laughed again, and it was one of those contagious laughs, which told everyone of his love for it: deep, heartfelt, and infectious. She liked him already for his laugh alone.

"You picked up on that, ay?"

"Educated guess."

There was silence before he explained. "Steve and I went to school together in Sydney, and we've stayed in contact."

She remembered Steve had grown up in Sydney but then moved to Melbourne in his early teens because of his father's job. Mat's voice brought her back from her thoughts, before she was able to reply.

"Darling, I love talking to you, but I've got to be somewhere in an hour. Can you promise me you'll be okay?"

"Thanks, Mat. Yes, I'll be fine." It wasn't a big lie, because at that moment she was feeling better.

She hung up and noticed a smile on her face. And instead of a churning stomach, butterflies had made themselves comfortable. She thought of how easy the conversation had flowed and how attentive he'd been. And his voice. She liked his voice. It was deep and calm, smooth and articulate. She closed her eyes and lost herself in his accent. It hadn't been strong, but still obvious to her.

And then there'd been his laugh. God, his laugh. It had turned her inside out.

With a big exhale, she covered her face with her hands, surprised that on a day she had to face the police, she was drooling over a man she'd never met, but only talked to.

For a mere few minutes, at that.

The police. A ripple of worry went through her, and she stood to search for her phone to give Steve another call. This time on his mobile.

****

The GPS voice in Matiu Apanui's car had as little of a clue as he did about the directions to get to his meeting place, and after half an hour, he was still on the western side of Melbourne instead of in the city. The reason for it was Tiffany, who was on the threshold of his thoughts. He replayed the phone conversation over and over in his head. It was clear something must've upset her. Even though she'd relaxed during their short conversation, he'd been able to sense her tension.

"Shit," he shouted as he pressed the speed dial button on his phone, remembering he'd never left a note for his friend.

"Mate, where are you?" Steve asked, by way of answering.

"I have no idea. Near a big park. Looks pretty with the trees alongside the walking tracks. Had no idea Melbourne had all these deciduous trees—"

"Mat!"

"The lovely GPS lady took me on a sightseeing tour first it seems. I'm considering stopping for a coffee and to reboot her at the same time."

"And you called me to tell me that?"

Mat noticed the frustration in his friend's voice and asked bluntly, "Tell me about your girlfriend."

There was a brief silence, before Steve asked, "You want to talk about Jess?"

Mat's laughter echoed in the small car as he turned off the engine and got out. With a few long strides, he headed towards the café. "I thought Jess is more than your girlfriend. I'm talking about Tiffany."

There was a groan on the other end of the line. "I heard about your phone call. You must've left some impression, but if you start any rumours by calling her my girlfriend I will kill you."

As he stepped inside the cafe, Mat asked, "You heard?"

"I've already spoken to her, but I don't—"

"I'm glad you did. Tiffany was desperate to talk to you. I hope you were able to help her."

Mat held his phone away for a moment, smiled at the young woman behind the counter, and ordered his coffee.

"You're still there?" Steve asked with a loud voice.

Mat shook his head with a smile and explained, "Yes, mate, just ordering a much-needed coffee." His friend's resigned sigh gave him another chuckle. "If you've already talked to her, we're all good, ay."

"We're all good. Thanks for calling anyway and good luck finding your way. But, by the way, what the hell did you two talk about?"

Mat took a sip of the coffee and was impressed by the flavour considering it cost him only a few bucks.

"Mat, you're pissing me off here. Will you focus on this conversation?"

"Geez, Steve. When did you get so touchy?"

There was a sharp intake of breath and an exhale on the other end of the line. "Tiff had a rough twelve months and a shitty morning. I'm simply concerned."

Mat froze mid-stride. Damn! He'd assumed something was wrong, but now he was curious about the history of it all. "What happened?"

"What the hell did you talk to her about, Matiu?" His friend's voice was now loud and his tone impatient.

Mat leaned against the car with one hand in his pocket and watched the heavy traffic, recalling his conversation with Tiffany earlier that day. "Well," he began. "I answered your phone, and she hung up but rang again. I told her you weren't home, and she asked me to leave a message and hung up. I returned the call, and we had a bit of a chit chat. You seem very overprotective."

There was a pause before Steve spoke. "Yeah, she's a great friend who's been through a rough patch."

"How come you've never talked about her?"

"I probably have mentioned her, but nothing worth you remembering."

"Should've though, I guess." Mat thought about it for a moment. "Anyway, glad you talked to her. The panic in her voice had me worried. You'll have to tell me more about your girl tonight. I've got to go," he said eventually with a grin.

"She's not my girl," his friend replied through gritted teeth. "And good luck with your meeting."

Mat disconnected the call, placed the cup of coffee on the top of the car, and tried to re-program the direction to his meeting place in his phone. How he missed Queenstown at that moment. With probably a mere tenth of Melbourne's population, navigation was easy, only hampered sometimes by tourists who drove on the wrong side of the road or who were simply lost.

He thought of Steve's comment about Tiffany's rough year. Worry shot through him, and he wished he'd copied her number to his phone.

The sound of her voice still played in his head. A tone that stoked angst and concern.

Exhaling a long breath, Mat focussed back to the problem at hand, got into the car, and listened to the GPS directions — as well as following them. Thankfully, within half an hour he found himself in an office opposite Karen Young, the representative of an Australian travel agency. A few months earlier, Mat had lost the coin toss between him and his partner Adam, and it was now he who was in Melbourne trying to negotiate a deal with Karen. Mat was interested in including his helicopter flights as part of a travel package for tourists in Queenstown, his hometown. He stepped into her small office, instantly overcome by some mild claustrophobia when he saw a small window with no view, but showing the walls of the building next door. Inhaling a breath, he forced himself to take in the rest of the well-decorated office, with framed photos from all over the world.

Including his beloved Queenstown.

Most of the places he knew, although he'd never been there, and he wondered whether Karen had.

"Nice meeting you, Mat."

He shook Karen's hand and was surprised by her firm grip. "Likewise."

As they sat, he studied her small frame, her short wavy grey hair, and soft blue eyes. He assumed her to be in her mid to late fifties. Her complexion was honey brown with not even a small blemish on her skin, but a few lines around her eyes.

Her assistant brought some coffee and biscuits.

"You've brought the cold weather to Melbourne," Karen said, as she poured herself some coffee. Pointing to his take-a-way coffee cup, she asked, "Would you like a fill-up?"

"I'm right, thanks," he replied, ignoring her swipe at the weather. Mat emptied his cup of coffee with one long sip before he placed it on the table. "Are you still going ahead with the contract?"

He was referring to the nasty incident a week earlier with a helicopter crash in the mountains. It'd been a big blow for the small communities of Fox and Franz Josef Glacier.

Karen nodded. "Terrible. Just terrible." She paused and leaned back in her chair. "Yes, we'd like to go ahead with the contract. We assume by the time you'll have set up the business in Queenstown, it will be out of the news."

Mat's stomach squeezed. How he hated this side of business. If this hadn't meant a big opportunity for him and Adam, he'd have cancelled the whole meeting. Bugger the money. But he wanted to move back to Queenstown and the contract would give him the finances to set up an office in his hometown.

Karen reached for her cup of coffee. "Tell me about you and your partner."

He leaned back into the chair and crossed his legs. It was his favourite subject. "Adam and I started our helicopter business five years ago in Fox Glacier. It was simple as we liked the idea of doing what we loved every day and meeting people from all over the world at the same time. Now we fly hundreds of tourists to the summit of the glacier or hunters and hikers to inaccessible huts on the top of the mountains."

"And what about the idea to move to Queenstown."

He cocked a brow. "We're not moving. Staff in Fox Glacier is brilliant. We're expanding at a nice rate. Now we'd like to expand to Queenstown. It's my hometown. I'd love to show off where I grew up."

"I can see why," she replied with a smile. "Okay then."

He gave a slow nod. "Okay. Let's talk figures."

Mat's knowledge about *figures* was basic and something he'd learnt over the last few years since he'd started the business with Adam. They hadn't been able to afford someone to look after their books, so they'd handled the task themselves. Yet, he knew what he wanted, and after two hours of discussing, arguing, and checking numbers, he'd finally come to an agreement with Karen on their first draft. It was now up to their lawyers to settle on the details.

Before he left, though, they spent another few minutes talking about New Zealand, travelling, and how he'd come to be a helicopter pilot. He liked Karen, and she promised she'd be one of the first to fly with him once he'd moved.

Mat walked back to his car, tired and worn out. Too much talking. When it came to the business side of things, his heart wasn't as invested. He loved flying, loved being up in the air, the sensation of no ties, and gazing at the wonders Mother Nature had to offer.

****

Tiffany walked down the floating wooden staircase, which reached up to her half-floor loft bedroom, and into the kitchen for a drink. Water gushed from the faucet as she filled the kettle and then switched it on.

Her mind returned to the conversation with Steve's friend, Mat. She'd enjoyed the brief, although bizarre, conversation. His voice had been so happy and full of energy it had taken her mind off her problem within only a few minutes. Something she hadn't been able to achieve with the bath she had taken later that morning. The whole hysteria from the previous year had crept up, leaving her anxious, tense, and with a headache. A nice cup of tea would hopefully do the trick. She thought of Mat's laugh and her mouth curled in response. It was deep and hearty. One of those laughs that could be contagious to anyone who heard it. Just thinking about it brought a smile to her lips. Closing her eyes, she tried to remember whether Steve had ever mentioned Mat's name, but as much as she tried, she wasn't able to recall ever hearing about a friend from New Zealand.

The whistling kettle drew her back from her thoughts, and she filled her cup. Dipping the teabag in and out of the water, she recalled her conversation with Steve earlier in the day when he'd finally returned her call.

"What's up, Tiff? I've got about three missed calls here," he had asked, not giving her a chance to even say hello.

Just hearing his voice sent a jolt of relief through her, almost catching her breath. After all, most of her problems weren't half as bad once Steve was there to help. Despite him being her brother Liam's best friend, Steve and Tiffany had become close during the year Liam had gone to London for a gap year.

"Why haven't you ever told me about Mat?" Stunned by her own question, she slapped her forehead a few times wondering where the question had come from — especially as matters more important were on hand.

There was a quiet chuckle on the other end of the line, and she was momentarily struck by a bout of embarrassment.

"Your problem can't be too bad," Steve replied with a hint of sarcasm.

Ignoring his comment, she said, "The police was here asking about Hudson."

Silence hung in the air before he replied, "Shit. No wonder I've had so many missed calls."

"Not to mention the amount of time I tried to get hold of you on your landline. So who the hell is this guy, and why did he answer your phone?"

"First things first, tell me about the police."

Tiffany headed into the lounge room and sat on the couch. "As I said already, they turned up here this morning wanting to know about Hudson."

"Why?"

She shrugged, but quickly added, "How the hell would I know?"

Her friend's sigh alerted her that frustration grew within him, so she told him about the visit earlier in the day in every detail. She looked around the lounge room as she spoke, taking in the bright colours of the painted walls, the small, but rustic fireplace, her sofa and matching armchairs, and the bookshelves, packed with books and photos.

"I'm sorry to bother you with this, but I don't know where else to go. Mum and Dad will worry themselves sick and won't be any use. And Liam will go berserk when he finds out the police came to the house again. I'm still glad he didn't get locked up when he pushed that officer last year. And there's also the fact that Mel's stress-o-meter is supposed to stay below zero."

There was silence at the other end of the line and a smile tugged at Tiffany's mouth, assuming he got her hint about Liam's wife.

"Run that by me again?" he finally asked.

"Focus, Steve. Focus. I need your help." Her smile turned into a grin despite anxiety spreading through her.

"Okay, I'll be there in half an hour. You can tell me all about Mel's stress levels on the way to the police."

"You first."

"First what?"

"You're first to reveal all about your Kiwi friend."

He snorted and hung up without replying.

Tiffany tried to eat something and although the sandwich in front of her looked delicious with the fresh cucumber, tomatoes, and ham, she wasn't able to take a bite. Impatient and unable to relax, she went into her bedroom and tidied up while thinking back to the time she had spent with Hudson.

She'd met him over a year ago. He'd been in her business management classes, and she'd liked him straight away. Sexy described him to the dot. His voice, his face, his sense of how to dress, his compliments…she was sure she could come up with more. Yet, his enthusiasm had been lacking, and he'd struggled through classes. Obviously, Tiffany had been happy to help, because hanging out with the wrong crowd, or friends as they called themselves, in school, she'd left after Year 9 with nowhere to go, and she knew how it was. Hudson and Tiffany hung out more and more, until they'd spent a night together. Rolling her eyes at herself, she admitted, yes, perfect was the right word to describe having sex with him. He'd known how and where to touch her, exploring every curve with his mouth, leaving a trail of kisses. The mere thought still sent shivers down her spine, followed by a chill thinking about what had happened the next day. She'd found him in his lounge room, all pale with little pearls of sweat on his forehead. It hadn't taken her long to figure out the reason for his distress. When she started giving him a lecture about drugs, he'd snapped, throwing a tantrum.

Her mistake had been to persist instead of leaving and closing the door on their short chapter. When she'd dared to shake her head in disgust, he clipped her across the jaw with a perfect fist. She'd fought hard to stay on her feet, ignoring the intense pain and the dizziness. It hadn't been a one off. Another hit...and next thing she remembered she'd woken up in hospital.

And now he was causing her trouble again. Though, not directly, it seemed.

An indescribable emotion grew inside her. She stared towards the window and watched the few birds in the back yard. Although anger and worry tried to trickle through her, the emotions inside her were more like an emptiness. It was as if Hudson had never existed during the last twelve months and giving him room inside her, in the form of any emotion, was something she wouldn't allow to happen.

And, yet, the police thought she had information that could help. Help with what? How? Did she have it in her to help?

When she heard a knock at the front door, she flinched and cursed the unknown situation grating so much on her nerves.

Opening the door for Steve, she gave him a grateful smile. As usual, he looked stunning with his suntanned face, his light green eyes, and just a shadow of a beard. His Irish red hair was a bit longer nowadays, which was most likely the current fashion, and Tiffany liked it. It gave him a sexier, yet mature look. Their friendship had grown even closer after her trouble with Hudson the previous year. He and Liam had been there for her when the police had knocked on her door and taken her to the station. It had been the worst period in her life. Both men had been by her side, though, caring for her and guiding her through the labyrinth of a legal nightmare.

He probably knew how anxious she was.

"Hi, Tiff," he said, as he placed a kiss on her cheek. "Sorry, we've got to rush a bit. Jessi and I have an appointment in the afternoon."

"Your girlfriend could show some—"

He held up his hand and his expression turned into a sly grin. "Let's say we have a situation where I want to keep her stress levels as low as possible."

She froze and a slow smile curved her lips. "Are you telling me there's going to be a little Steve junior?"

"I'm telling you we're having an appointment and that we've got to hurry along a bit."

"How exciting." Tiffany grabbed her keys, locked the door, and followed him to his car.

Once they were buckled up and on the road, Steve asked, "Have you had any contact with Hudson since?"

"No way. Once bitten, twice shy. Isn't that what they say?" She tucked a strand of hair behind her ear and sat straight. "Okay, distract me a bit and tell me about Mat."

He shook his head. "Sounds like love at first sight. Or *hear*, I suppose."

"Oh, my God, no, but I'm curious about him."

He chuckled. "Mat lived across the road from us in Sydney," he explained with a shrug. "His dad had been a famous rugby player in New Zealand. The family moved to Sydney where his dad did some coaching. None of them really settled, though. Mat and I stayed in contact since. Liam and I visited him numerous times. I'm hoping to invest in his new business venture. That's why he's here."

"What kind of business?"

Steve parked and turned to look at her. "How about a barbeque at our place tomorrow night? I'm sure he'll be more than happy to tell you all about his little barn in the middle of nowhere."

"Barn?"

He laughed. "He bought the thing a few years back and turned it into one mighty great house. Shame he's moving back to Queenstown."

They got out of the car and walked towards the police station entrance. A sudden rush of anxiety swept through her, leaving her hands cold and her heart pounding in her throat.

Taking her hand, Steve said, "You'll be right. I'm sure there's a simple explanation to it."

She let out a puff of air. "With the police ending up at my doorstep wanting information about Hudson, I doubt the explanation is simple."

Two

TWENTY minutes later, Tiffany and Steve sat in a small, barren room opposite Senior Constable Jones and Sergeant Harris. In an effort to calm her nerves, Tiffany tried hard to control her shaking body with a few slow and deep breaths, but to no avail. She was shivering as if she was freezing, and her skin was cold and clammy.

The officers introduced themselves to Steve.

"Good meeting you," Steve said. "I'm Steve Casey, and a good friend of Tiffany's."

Tiffany looked over to him, grateful for his company.

Harris leaned forward, placing his elbows on the table. "I'd like to clarify again this is purely a conversation to collect information. Miss Cahill is free to reply to questions at her will. Nothing will be recorded."

Steve looked at Tiffany, giving her an almost imperceptible nod.

"Okay," she replied to Harris.

"You knew Thomas Terrill as Hudson?" Jones asked, as she slid a photo across the table towards Tiffany.

She nodded.

"You were in a relationship at the time?"

"A brief encounter is what I'd call it."

Harris met her gaze, acknowledging her reply, then asked, "When did you see him last?"

"About a year ago."

"Why did you stop the contact?"

"The evil bastard beat me into unconsciousness."

Although both Harris and Jones kept their expressions straight, Tiffany was sure she saw something like surprise and sympathy on Jones' face.

"After that?"

She shook her head.

"We have a file note regarding an incident a few weeks later."

Steve placed a hand on her shoulder and ran it up and down her back in a soothing stroke, calming her with a slight rhythmic move. Tiffany let out a long breath.

"Not one of the police's finest moments," she said, trying hard to convey some humour when she didn't feel any.

Harris met her gaze, but remained silent.

Closing her eyes, she said, "If it's all in a file, I suppose it's not necessary for me to retell the details, is it?"

"Any contact with Thomas after that incident?"

She shook her head again. "Thankfully, no."

"Ever talked to anybody about him?"

Her eyes shot open and with a shrug, she replied, "Possibly my brother, but I doubt it. Hudson's not worth wasting even a second of my life on. Hard to believe I'm here because of him."

"To your knowledge, would your brother have talked to anybody about him?"

"I'd say no for the very same reason. Got him into enough trouble last year."

Harris nodded. "Miss Cahill. How good is your knowledge of cars?"

Surprised by the question, she hesitated. "Next to nothing," she replied with a frown.

"Would you know where to find the brake cable?"

She shrugged. "I had no idea there was a cable. Isn't it just the foot pedal?"

Harris smiled and looked at Steve. "Have you ever met Thomas Terrill?"

"No, sir," Steve said without hesitation. "Didn't know him in person."

Jones took the photo, and Harris sat back. "Mr. Thomas Terrill was killed in a car accident last week. Although we found drugs in the car, Mr. Terrill's blood test came back negative. However…" He paused for a moment, possibly letting all the information sink in before he continued. "We found the brake cable had been tampered with. If you know or can think of anything that might assist our investigation, we'd appreciate you telling us."

She stared at him, taking in every single word. Was Harris implying murder? Hudson was murdered? She thought for a long moment, trying to process the information. "At the moment, I cannot think of anything, most likely because of the uncomfortable situation of being here." Pulling out the business card he'd given her earlier in the day, she held it up and added, "But I will give you a call if something comes to mind."

"Please do."

After a few more pleasantries, they all stood and shook hands. The relief that washed over Tiffany as soon as she exited the room was so intense, it left her dizzy, and she held on to Steve for a moment.

"Are you all right?"

"It's the adrenaline causing me a rush of light-headedness."

"Need a drink of water?"

"No. Just let's get the hell out of here. Can't say it's a place I like."

He chuckled as he checked his watch.

"And you have the appointment to check on Junior."

Steve placed an arm around her shoulder and with a soft tug pulled her closer to him. Placing a kiss on her forehead, he said against her skin, "I'll kill you if you spill the beans to anybody."

"Yes, honey. My lips are sealed."

As soon as they stepped out of the building, Tiffany said, "I'll get the bus home. There's a bus stop only a few minutes from here."

"Sure?"

She nodded and moved out of his arm. "A hundred percent. You better get to the appointment."

"I owe you."

Shaking her head, she replied, "No you don't. I wouldn't even know how to thank you for coming along today."

He took her head into his hands and placed another kiss on her forehead. "Promise me you'll be fine on that bus."

"Hudson's dead, remember."

"Yes, but the way it sounds it's not by choice."

"What are you saying?"

He met her eyes. "Yes, what am I saying? More importantly, why did I say it?" With a shrug, he added, "The whole thing doesn't sit well with me, but I suppose I worry too much. Or so I'm told. I'd better go. Don't forget the barbeque tomorrow."

A smiled tugged at her lips. "Can't wait."

Tiffany walked to the bus stop with Steve's words playing on her mind. *Not by choice.* Obviously someone had killed Hudson, aka Thomas Terrill. And, why the two different names?

She exhaled a long breath when she saw the bus coming around the corner. Quickly, she retrieved her card and stepped back.

Not by choice.

A shiver ran down her spine, and she tentatively looked around, not knowing, what she was looking for.

Damn the police for involving her in this mess, and damn Steve for making that remark.

****

Mat loosened his tie and undid the top button of his shirt as soon as he entered the room he'd been staying in at Steve's. Relieved about the outcome of the meeting with Karen, he kicked off his shoes and threw himself onto the bed while dialling Adam's number in New Zealand.

"Kia Ora[1], my friend. What's the news?"

Mat smiled. "We've got the deal. It's now up to the lawyers to negotiate the big money."

"Ka Mau te Wehi![2]"

Mat rolled his eyes at his friend's terrible mispronunciation of the Maori words. "Will you stop that, please?"

Adam's bark of laughter echoed through the phone. It was days like these when he regretted teaching his friend the language. Unlike Mat, whose background was half Maori, half English, and his command of the Maori and English languages fluent, Adam's parents had moved to New Zealand thirty years ago when he had been a baby.

"I like it," Adam replied, a chuckle still in his voice. "You won't be able to teach me for much longer once you move to Queenstown."

Queenstown. Despite looking forward to moving to the bigger city, his stomach still churned every time he thought about leaving his friend behind. But Adam had settled with his wife just outside Fox Glacier and they were expecting their first child at the end of the year. It was time for Mat to move on, and he was excited about the challenge to extend their business.

---

[1] Hello.

[2] That's great.

Mat gave Adam all the details of the meeting before he hung up. He tapped the phone against his chin as his chat with the mysterious Tiffany drifted into his thoughts. He shut his eyes for a second as he recalled their conversation. Her voice. Her frustration. Or had it been fear?

He lowered his phone and dialled Steve's number. The phone rang a few times then went to voice mail. Raking his hand through his short hair, another thought came to him, and he got up in search of Steve's home phone.

It must've been his lucky day. Tiffany's number was stored in the speed dial. Hesitating, he eventually pushed the button and his heartbeat soared with each ringtone, until she finally answered.

"Darling, please tell me you're going to have a little girl."

Mat cocked a brow, not sure how to respond. "Should I even bother asking what this is about?"

"What is it with you using Steve's phone?" she asked, her voice an octave or two higher than this morning.

He gave her a bemused smile. "I was worried about you and wanted to check whether you're all right?"

There was a moment of silence. "You need to forget that first question, okay?" she almost begged in a whisper.

"Will do. I think if you share a pizza with me, it'll make it easier to forget."

Another moment of silence. This one was longer, though, and he wondered if he'd pushed it too far.

"Are you blackmailing me?"

"Nope, only hoping to meet you."

"For all you know, I could be a bitch. And ugly. And absolutely… absolutely…I could be gay."

"I'd still like to have this pizza to make sure you're okay," he said, surprising himself by his own words, because, truth be told, it wasn't his thing to date bitchy women or ugly ones for that matter. As for the gay bit, he doubted that very much, otherwise Steve would've dropped a hint.

A little laugh escaped her lips. "No wonder the All Black's just won the World Cup. Persistence seems to be part of your genes."

"Oh, Tiffany. You like rugby?" He almost drooled.

"With a football-mad-brother I'm not allowed to like any other sport," she explained with some cheeriness.

He loved the laughter in her voice. And even though there was still the reason she'd been so upset earlier in the day, he was glad he was able to put a little happiness in her voice.

"Are you comfortable enough to give me your address or would you like to meet at the pizza place down the street from here."

She hesitated. "The pizzeria sounds like a good idea. I could be there in about an hour."

Excited, he replied, "Deal. I look forward to meeting you."

She laughed. "This is about the weirdest thing ever. Don't bring a rose, though. You'll recognise me when you see a very nervous person coming in."

"No rose. Got it."

Mat hung up and made a little fist pump in the air. It wasn't his first date, so it surprised him how nervous he was. In fact, it wasn't a date, but a meeting to find out more about Tiffany and to put his mind at ease. After all, she really had sounded distressed earlier that morning.

He had a quick shower and towelled himself off before getting dressed in his jeans, grey shirt, and black shoes. He tried to get hold of Steve on the phone, but again was instructed to leave a message. "Mate, I'm out for dinner. Will catch up with you later. Ka kite.[3]"

---

[3] See you (Bye)

One last check of the time, and he decided it was late enough to leave. The pizzeria was indeed only down the road, so he walked the short distance. As soon as he stepped into the restaurant, the smell of freshly baked pizza, garlic, and fire assaulted him, making his mouth water.

Mat looked around, liking the typical ambience of an Italian eatery. The wooden tables were covered with white and red checked tablecloths, white plates decorated with a green napkin each, and some crunchy breadsticks in a clear glass vase in the centre of the table.

An empty table in the far corner seemed to have a good view of the entrance. After a brief eye contact with the waiter, he made his way to the table, still surprised at the events that led him here.

It wasn't more than five minutes when a woman entered through the door. Mat knew straight away it was Tiffany and smiled when their eyes met.

Her lips curved into a smile as well, and his whole body was suddenly on alert.

Three

TIFFANY knew the man in the corner was Mat as soon as she looked at him. In her mind, his smile matched his laugh.

Yet, she double-checked and stole a quick look around just to be certain, but she wasn't able to find another single man occupying a table. Her gaze fell back on Mat, who stood as she slowly walked towards him. There was an awkward silence in the air, briefly broken by the noise from the kitchen.

"Tiffany?"

She nodded, unable to speak, a thousand words running through her head, none of them making it to her vocal cords, though. And although her mind was still occupied by the saga with the police, during the occasional moments she'd thought about Mat she'd envisioned him to be the complete opposite. Looking at him, she knew he was trouble.

Good trouble.

Sexy trouble.

And thank goodness, he was from New Zealand, and most likely to return home soon, because she didn't need trouble. Whether it was good or sexy. But damn, he had a body to die for. His black hair was cut short, his brown almond eyes alive with interest as he held her gaze.

They sat in silence, Tiffany still a bit overwhelmed by the situation. And Mat's looks.

"Would you like a drink?" he asked at long last.

She nodded and was glad to get a "Cola please" over her lips.

There was a thin scar visible in his hairline, and she wondered what'd happened. When Mat lifted his arm to get the waiter's attention, she noticed a tattoo on his arm, which disappeared under his shirt, but she assumed it was a Maori tattoo, which usually spread across the shoulder as well. His eyes and bronze skin told her he was probably of Maori origin.

He ordered their drinks and met her gaze again with a smile. It took her a lot of effort not to shiver with lust.

"It's nice meeting you," he said and smiled, revealing two small dimples in his cheek.

She let out a little laugh. "I still can't believe I'm here."

A broad grin crossed his face, and he winked at her. "I'm glad you came."

Tiffany exhaled a shaky breath. "Okay, tell me a bit about you."

Mat snorted. "No way. You'll run away."

"That bad?" she asked with a smile.

"Worse."

"I can't believe that."

Warmth spread across his face. "What would you like to know?"

She thought about it. Not wanting to sound too eager, she asked, "Tell me about your tattoo. And your necklace—I like it."

Cocking a brow, he moved his shirt up a little. "My tattoo?"

"I didn't want to sound like a mother and ask for your life's history."

He shook his head as he laughed. "Technically, it's a ta moko. It's part of my Maori background. It used to be a tribal thing."

"Is the necklace a tribal thing as well?"

"Don't know much about your neighbours across the sea, do you?"

She gave a little shrug. "Never had a need to."

"The pounamu toki is a symbol of strength and courage."

Tiffany reached out and carefully held it with her thumb and finger. "I love it. It's beautiful." She met his gaze. "You're proud of your heritage, aren't you?"

He choked back a chuckle. "What makes you say that?"

"Not sure, but I get a feeling you're not wearing it for show. It means something to you."

"It's what I am. I'm proud of what I am." Mat took her hand in his. "Tell me what upset you this morning."

The waiter brought their drinks, and she slowly removed her hand from his.

"How about we order dinner, ay?" he suggested.

They both ordered a pizza, hers a Hawaiian, Mat chose an Aussie classic, and for a moment their conversation shifted to Steve and how each of them knew him. Mat told her a mirror story of Steve's about their years in Sydney.

"I went to Sydney a few years back, but it was way too hectic for me," she told him with a sigh.

"It's a great place, but it's not NZ," he replied.

"Steve told me your dad used to play rugby."

He nodded. "He was an All Black."

"Why didn't you follow in his footsteps?"

Raising a brow, he leaned back to let the waiter place their meals on the table before he replied, "Everyone expected me to be like my dad. I wanted to be me."

Tiffany took a piece of her pizza, pondering his statement. And liked it. For so long she'd competed with her successful brother, resulting in giving up and leaving school early. It had only been the last few years that she'd realised what she was, all she had become, was because of her own doings, and it wasn't about competing, but becoming the best at her abilities. That was when she'd started the business management night classes.

"And what is it you do?" she asked.

"I'm a helicopter pilot."

"Damn," she exclaimed. "That's not even close to rugby."

He laughed as he lifted his glass to take a sip of his drink. "What about you?"

"My life's boring. Not much to tell."

He chuckled. "Boring? I have a feeling it's quite the opposite. Come on. Let me be the judge of it. I know nothing about you except that you're Steve's friend, close friend. How do you know him?"

"He's Liam's best friend."

He raised his brows enquiringly. "You know Liam?"

"Liam's my brother. How do you know him?"

A frown appeared on his face. "How well do you know your brother? He came over for a visit with Steve a few years back."

"I vaguely remember him travelling to Auckland while I was away."

"Vaguely?"

"I spent three years travelling around Australia. As much as Mum and Dad tried to keep me up-to-date, they were vague on details."

He nodded. "Three years on the road. Sounds like a great adventure. My brother had the same intentions at some stage, but life took over."

"You have a brother? Younger or older?"

A grin stretched across his face. "Nice try. Back to your life."

"Sorry." She paused and blew out a breath. "It's an odd story. A bit complicated as well. And doesn't leave me in a good light, I suppose."

Lifting his knife, he joked, "Killed someone?"

She looked past him towards the window to avoid his gaze. Out of the corner of her eye, she saw him placing his knife next to his plate before he rested his elbows on the table.

"The trouble this morning?"

Nodding, she bit her lower lip, worried he'd judge her. She wasn't ready, yet, to not see him again. She studied his face, almost drowning in his eyes. He seemed so perfect in so many ways. Hudson had seemed so perfect, too.

And it scared her somewhat.

****

From the moment Tiffany had walked into the restaurant, Mat had an inkling that she wasn't gay or a bitch for that matter. Not only did she look gorgeous in her plain tight jeans, a simple white T-shirt, and her kick-arse short haircut, but also her smile was genuine and bright, her blue eyes radiated peace and happiness — except when he'd asked whether she'd killed someone. Not for a second did he believe, though, that she'd killed someone. Her demeanour said differently. Tilting his head, he watched her avoiding his stare, biting her lips as she ran her fingers through her short hair, undoubtedly messing it up.

"Bad?"

Their eyes met again. "No. Not bad. A person I knew was killed and the circumstances...well, less than pleasant."

"Accident?"

She snorted. "I'd say."

"In a selfish way, I'm glad I've been able to put a little smile on your beautiful face."

It didn't get past him that her cheeks flushed a little, and he bit back a grin at his achievement.

"We both have brothers. We both have Steve as a great friend. We both like rugby…"

She laughed. "I know next to nothing about rugby. I know the All Blacks are from New Zealand, and they won the world cup."

"Okay, fair enough. But you like sports."

"More watching than being active. I like the occasional swim."

"Lucky me. At the end of the dinner, I might be able to convince you to take me to a beautiful beach for a swim."

Now her laugh was half a snort. "Without a doubt, All Black persistence."

"Job?"

"Yes and no."

He cocked a brow.

"I'm studying for my Diploma in Business Management. And some nights I work at the pub to get some extra cash."

Taking a sip from his drink, he eyed her over the rim. "Business management," he said, setting his glass on the table. "Impressive."

"Not even close to as impressive as being a helicopter pilot," she said, yet not looking at him.

Mat became more and more intrigued by her. Her shy nature, the self-doubt that shone through when talking about herself, and the hesitation to tell him more about the person she was.

"Born in Melbourne?"

"Yes, born and raised in Melbourne. You?"

"Born in Queenstown, lived in Auckland most of my life, and moving to Queenstown soon."

"North or south island?"

"Auckland is north, Queenstown is south."

"New Zealand must be beautiful. I've never been there."

Mat grinned, knowing too well, she'd changed the subject away from her again. But he didn't push it any further and started telling her about New Zealand, a subject close to his heart he could've talked about for days. He enjoyed her company, her interest in most things, and the way she soaked up each of his words.

A couple of hours later, Tiffany checked her phone, and said, "I'm really sorry, but it's time for me to go, but I will see you at Steve's barbeque tomorrow, right?"

Mat nodded. "Wouldn't miss it for the world."

They stood, and he went to pay for the dinner before he joined Tiffany outside.

"Can I walk you to your car?"

With a soft laugh, she said, "It's right there," pointing at a red little car about twenty metres up the road. He groaned inwardly, knowing his time with her was about to be over. Placing his hand on the small of her back, they started walking the few metres in silence. Once they got to the car, Tiffany dug in her bag for the keys and pushed the remote to unlock it.

"Thanks for a nice evening," she said just above a whisper. "It was just what I needed after a shitty day."

It took all his courage, but he leaned in and gently touched her lips with his. Her soft breath touched his skin and teased his sanity. The taste of cola still lingered on her lips, and he was tempted to kiss her with all he had and all he felt at that moment. An undercurrent of attraction made him aware of how much he'd enjoyed their time together and how much he disliked letting her go already. He leaned back to meet her gaze and, although pleased, it surprised him she didn't move back or slap his cheek. Unsure about her expression, he was confident, though, that there was no anger, but a hesitant smile, that made him want to kiss her again.

"Can't wait to see you again tomorrow."

Her cheeks turned a soft shade of red.

"Will you be all right?" he asked.

Her eyes widened. "Because I've been kissed by a stranger?"

Not able to hold back, he burst into a bark of laughter. "I'm good, but even I know a touch of my lips is nothing that moves the earth." He paused, watching her expression. "I meant in regard to what happened this morning."

The long sigh she emitted almost told the whole story, and he wished instead of bringing it up he had kissed her again.

"Someone died under suspicious circumstances, and the police came to see me this morning. I freaked out."

She held his stare, most likely wanting to see his reaction. And in all fairness, it wasn't at all what he'd expected. Possibly — but then again, he didn't know what he'd expected either, yet the mention of the word police threw him a bit.

"You're not a suspect, are you?" he asked with a little jest in his voice not believing that was the case.

Her gaze went past him as she shook her head. He cupped her chin with both hands, tilting her head towards him to see her eyes. Sadness had taken over, and he could've kicked himself for his curiosity.

He drew a deep breath. "Sorry."

"No. Don't be. You did nothing wrong." With a slight lift of her shoulder, she added, "We dated for a very brief time before it ended. His name kind of left a sour taste in my mouth, so I'm still torn between not caring and feeling sorry for him."

Mat pulled out his wallet from the back pocket of his pants and retrieved one of his business cards.

"My number's on here. Promise me you'll call me if you need to talk."

Tiffany's lips parted as she reached for the card, but she didn't say anything. Her hesitation was obvious when she paused before taking it. "I'm fine," she replied with a slight smile.

"Promise me," he insisted.

"Yes, Dad," she mocked. "I promise I will call you if for any reason I will need to talk to someone."

"'Atta girl."

"But first let me win the lotto, because this would be an overseas call."

A frown creased his forehead. "Shit! Never even thought about that."

She let out a soft laugh, but remained silent.

"Call through, and I will return the call," he suggested.

"I will, but honestly, I'm sure I'll be fine."

With no more words, she slid behind the steering wheel, and he closed the door. She started the engine and drove off, leaving him staring after her until she was completely out of sight. A few seconds later, he headed the opposite direction and started to walk back to Steve's house.

Slowly, and with a constant smile on his face.

He had another three days in Melbourne and hoped to see as much as possible of Tiffany during that time.

And a phone call later that night. That'd be the icing on the cake.

The lights in the house told Mat Steve was still awake. He unlocked the front door and followed the voices to the lounge room. Steve and Jessica were watching television. Mat experienced a moment of awkwardness as he entered his friend's house after spending the last three hours with Tiffany. The solitude of his own house would've been much preferred.

He looked around the room, noticing the female touch to the decor. A few more framed photos sat on the fireplace mantel, a few more cushions on the lounge, the curtains seemed to have more frill than before, the carpet was new, and there were certainly more books on the shelf.

"How are you?" he asked, as he sat on the single seater next to Steve. It didn't get past him that his friend sported a big grin. But then again, he probably did, too.

"How was dinner?" Jessica asked. "I'm sorry you had to go out."

He shook his head. "Nah. I went to the pizzeria down the street."

"Alone?" Steve asked, as he grabbed his beer from the table.

With a chuckle, he replied, "Tiffany."

Jessica's eyes widened. "Tiffany Cahill? You know her?"

"She called here this morning. Very persistently if I may say, so I answered."

She gave Steve a quick look, and Mat wasn't sure what to make of it. But he continued. "She seemed upset. We got to talking. So when I returned from my meeting this afternoon, I wanted to check whether she was okay. One thing led to another with us ending up meeting at the pizza place."

Jessica turned to Steve again. "What was wrong?"

"The police stopped by this morning. Hudson is dead. They had a few questions."

"Who's Hudson?" Mat asked.

"A guy she knew. Didn't end well."

"The one who died under suspicious circumstances?"

Steve's eyebrow raised a notch. "She told you?"

Mat shook his head. "Not in detail. It's easier to intimidate someone with the Haka than getting information out of Tiffany."

Jessica snorted, and Steve replied, "She had a rough time."

Again, Mat wasn't sure what to make of Jessica's gesture. Jealousy? Didn't she like her? Was there more to the story than Steve let on? But why wouldn't his friend tell him?

"But you can't tell me about it?"

He took a sip of his beer before he replied, "It's not for me to tell you."

Mat understood and respected his friend's reasoning. With a nod, he stood and headed to the kitchen where he snagged a cold drink from the fridge. He twisted the top off the bottle and took a swig. The beer sent a cool rush through his stomach and a shiver down his spine. He thought of Tiffany. How could he not? She was constantly on his mind, her little smile, or her curiosity and interest in so many things. Like his Maori background or what it was like to fly, to be in the air. Two subjects he loved and was able to talk about all the time. Usually, girls cared more about his business and the finances than his love for his job.

Jessica came into the kitchen and placed her cup in the sink. "Good night, Mat. Hope your meeting with the tourist people was successful."

A smile tugged at his lips. "It was, thank you. It's more or less a done deal."

"That's good. Congratulations. I suppose that means you're moving to Queenstown now?"

He nodded. "Yes, that's the plan."

She picked up the cup again and gave it a rinse. After she'd placed her cup in the sink again, she turned her head and met his gaze. "Tiffany is Steve's good friend, and I trust his judgement." The click-clack of her shoes echoed through the kitchen as she walked to the door with slow steps. She reached the door and placed her hand on the doorjamb, staying like that for several moments as though pondering whether or not to say anything. "I still remember seeing Tiff all beaten up in hospital. It's not something I'll forget any time soon. So, whenever she comes to Steve with a problem, I worry. Most likely for nothing, yet, I still do." She let out a long sigh and left.

Mat lifted the beer to his lips, but suddenly the taste and urge was gone, so he tipped it out, called a *goodnight* down the hall, and headed to his room.

There was so much more about Tiffany he didn't know.

In fact, he hardly knew her at all, and yet, she was all he could think about. He considered giving Adam another call, but in the end, he threw off his shoes before lying on the bed. With his legs crossed at the ankle and his hands behind his head, he daydreamt for a while, thinking about his new house in Queenstown. He'd bought the place a few weeks earlier, knowing he wanted it the minute he'd stepped inside. There were a few renovations needed, but he was happy to get that organised or do it himself. The house had a European ski chalet look to it with five rooms, but the flat terrace overlooking the lake and the mountains was all he'd needed to see to make an offer. There was a massive shed and a nice garage as well, ideal for all his gear.

And as he envisioned what kind of renovations he had in mind, he imagined Tiffany sitting outside on the terrace with a can of cola in her hand.

He sat up, rubbing his hands over his face, stunned by how much she occupied his mind. Unable to forget the simple touch of her lips on his.

He leaned back into the pillow again, aware of that constant grin on his face.

Four

TIFFANY parked in the driveway and fumbled with her keys on her way to the back door. A smile tugged at her lips as she heard the next-door neighbour on the drums again. He'd improved a lot over the last twelve months, and she often had the best intentions to ask him whether he'd played in a band. But life always got in the way.

Walking past the roses next to her bedroom window, she made a mental note to give them some water the next day. Her father always told her that nice front and back yards made up about a third of the property value. She'd laughed at him, but the longer she lived in her own house, the more she appreciated his words.

She inserted the key into the door when someone suddenly appeared out of nowhere, pulling her head backwards. Tiffany's heart rate spiked, and her head nearly exploded because of the rush of adrenalin through her body, the instant fear, and the shock of the situation she was in. Her instinct told her to fight, but when the tip of a knife touched her throat, barely skimming her skin, she stood still. Frozen.

Cursing Hudson.

And herself for getting involved with him in the first place. Panic raged inside her, fear running rampant through her veins. Her mind was still spinning at the thought that she hadn't seen or noticed the person in her driveway. He'd come out of nowhere like a ghost in a movie, taking her by surprise.

"Where's the list?" he asked with a deep voice.

A thousand thoughts rushed through her head, yet none of them of any use. Again, she cursed the hell out of Hudson. He had to be the reason for this. It'd be too much of a coincidence otherwise.

"I have no idea what you're talking about," she croaked.

The guy jerked her back by her hair, making it hard for her to swallow.

"Don't fuck with me."

The first tear ran down her cheek, and she tried hard to control the spasmodic trembling within her. "Please, you need to give me some kind of hint what you're after, otherwise we're not getting anywhere."

Surprised by her own words and reasoning, she tried to breathe in and out to calm herself. It'd been over a year now since Hudson had beaten her up to the extent that she'd spent three days in hospital. After that, she'd promised herself she'd never be the victim again. Unfortunately, she'd never imagined herself threatened with a knife at her throat.

"What's on the list? And who would have given it to me?" she rasped.

His snort was vile, his voice held an undertone of cold contempt. "Don't fuck with me. I saw Hudson coming here."

"He's dead."

Another jerk at her hair made her scream, which resulted in him pressing the knife even harder against her throat.

"Shut up," he warned her, his breath touching her ears, causing her stomach acid to rise up her throat.

"Here's how it goes," he whispered, his voice void of any emotion. "I don't care what you do or how you do it, but if I don't have that list by tomorrow, you will join Hudson six feet under." Yanking her head back again, he threatened, "Understood?"

Not able to move her head, Tiffany croaked a quiet, "Yes."

The force with which he let go of her head and pushed her away from him was so sudden Tiffany wasn't able to stop herself from knocking right into the door. The instant pain was so intense it was hard for her to breathe.

With a trembling hand, she inserted the key into the door lock and turned it before rushing inside and slamming it behind her. Tears now flowing in full force, she slid down the wall, not trusting her shaky legs. Yet, as she bowed her head forward, she uttered a string of curses, when a sudden urge made her cover her mouth with her hand. As quick as she was able to, she crawled to the toilet and threw up.

Over and over again until she was dry heaving.

Light-headed, she leaned back, drawing deep breaths through her nose until she was able to feel her heart rate settling. She closed her eyes, trying hard not to faint.

The silence around her weighed heavy on her, the only sound her own breathing. Time stood still, with Tiffany unable to form a thought or move.

After what seemed like hours, she crawled back to her bag and grabbed her mobile and the phone number she was given earlier that day.

With trembling hands, she dialled the number and waited for an answer.

"Hi, it's Tiffany Cahill here."

"How can I help you, Miss Cahill?" Sergeant Harris asked.

She wasn't able to get out a single word, but instead started sobbing uncontrollably.

"What happened?" he demanded.

Her head was aching, her eyes burning, her body shaking, and her mind full of words and details she wanted to tell him.

But no word came across her lips.

Instead, she sobbed even more.

"Tiffany," he said, his voice low and calming. "Try to answer yes or no." He paused. "Are you all right?"

The question seemed ridiculous to her, but she croaked, "No."

"Are you at home?"

"Yes."

"Alone?"

"Yes."

"Injured?"

She touched her throat but didn't feel any blood. "No."

"I'll be there in twenty minutes."

"Yes."

He disconnected the call and another wave of relief hit her. Weak and sore, she tried to stand and step-by-step moved to the kitchen where she got herself a glass of water. The cold fluid eased the pain of the acid in the back of her throat, soothed and cooled her parched mouth.

She forced her heavy legs to move and made it to the lounge room where she collapsed onto the sofa. A sense of loneliness spread through her as she picked up the phone, hesitating to call her brother. Hesitating to call Steve.

Another wave of nausea hit her as she realised how much she'd pushed people away over the last year, ending up on the couch alone after being assaulted by a stranger.

She closed her eyes, trying to empty her mind of all the negative thoughts and steady her breathing.

When the doorbell rang a little while later, Tiffany flinched at the shrill sound echoing through the quiet house. A quick glance at the clock told her that it'd been fifteen minutes since she'd called the police. Her shoulders tightened as she stepped to the window and risked a quick peek outside.

It was Sergeant Harris.

Almost dizzy with relief, she headed to the door. Without unhooking the security chain, she slowly opened the door and glanced through the small gap.

"You're on your own?" she asked.

"Will that be a problem? Senior Constable Jones is off duty."

Uncertain about letting him in, she was reluctant to open the door any farther.

"Are you alone?"

She nodded.

"Someone you can call? Family?"

"My brother, but I'd rather have a chance to tell him all about it first."

"Your friend from this morning?"

"He's pregnant."

He raised his eyebrow slightly.

"His girl is. Obviously not him."

He stepped back and pulled out a little notepad. "Okay. Tell me what happened?"

Taken aback by his action, she asked, "Is this putting you in an awkward situation?"

Raising a brow, he asked, "Why?"

She shrugged. "I'm sorry I called you. I came home about an hour ago, parked my car, walked to the back door, and as I was about to go inside, someone came out of nowhere and…"

She choked back a sob, trying hard to remember in detail what had happened. The words, his breath, and his voice were still stored in her head, and she was about to throw up again. As accurately as possible, she recapped the incident.

"Did you get to see him?"

She bit her lip and murmured, "No."

Again, he raised a brow, questioning her. "Did you say it happened at the back door?"

"Yes," she whispered.

"And you didn't see him leave?"

Biting the inside of her cheek, she tried to remember that moment. She rubbed her hands over her face, frustrated for not being able to recall more, but also to banish the unwanted emotions and images out of her head. "No, I was focussed on getting into the house."

He nodded and scribbled another few notes.

"Okay, you can't call your brother or your friend. Is there anybody else you could stay with tonight?"

The noise of the door chain caught her attention, and she noticed how she'd absentmindedly fidgeted with it. She stared past him when she finally replied, "I can stay with my mum and dad." Although the thought caused a wave of anxiety within her. How on earth would she explain the whole situation to her parents?

Her relationship with them had never been easy, especially with her father, who'd had different plans for her career. Travelling around Australia hadn't been his idea of a solid lifestyle. But she'd had fun for three years exploring the beauty of the country, the people, and various opportunities. Fortunately, when she'd come back to start what her father would've called a *serious life*, they'd helped her financially and paid for the deposit on her house. Since then, she'd survived by taking various jobs to pay the mortgage while studying business management. It was one of her parents' conditions when giving her the money. It'd been several tough years, but she was close to finishing her degree.

She would've been even closer if she hadn't had the hiccup with Hudson.

It'd been since leaving Hudson that her relationship with her parents had improved. Tiffany doubted though, it was good enough for her mother not to freak out when she'd hear about the reason for Tiffany's overnight stay.

She couldn't tell her mother the real reason.

Then again, her body would tell the story without her.

A small sigh escaped her lips.

"We have a safe house north of Melbourne. I could try to get you in there?"

Sergeant Harris tried so hard to help her, and suddenly she felt guilty for not letting him into her house.

A safe house? Was that her final choice? Staying in a strange house? With other people, none of them familiar to her?

Then, as she was about to agree to his suggestion, Mat popped into her head.

"Actually, I do know someone I could call."

"Very good."

A smile pulled at her lips. She met his gaze and decided to unhook the chain.

"Would you like to come in? I'll give him a call while you're here."

"I appreciate that you feel you can trust me, but considering there's no female officer with me, I'd rather you give him a call while I wait here."

Running a hand through her hair, she looked past him again. The idea to call Mat and ask him to come seemed as absurd as rejecting the suggestion to stay in a safe house. She didn't know Mat, except for the couple of hours she'd spent with him having dinner. Yet, she'd met him and talked to him. Most importantly, though, he was Steve's friend and had been close to twenty years. That fact should outrank the safe house by miles.

After she'd tossed and turned the ups and downs of calling Mat, she grabbed her phone and the little note with Mat's phone number from the lounge room. With her hands still shaking, or shaking again at the thought she was about to call her new Kiwi friend again...yet not under the circumstances she'd hoped for.

As she waited for the call to connect, she walked back to the front door with the police officer still waiting patiently.

"Hello?"

"Hi, it's Tiffany—"

Before she was able to finish the sentence, he interrupted her. "Hang up, darling, I'll call you right back."

She stared at the phone when she heard the busy dial tone.

"Not available?"

Before she was able to explain the situation, the phone buzzed, and she pushed the green button without delay.

"Hi," she answered, well aware that Sergeant Harris was listening.

"I was hoping for..."

"Are you able to come over? There's a situation here, and I don't want to trouble my brother or Steve, because...well, because of the situation I shouldn't tell you."

"Are you all right?" His concern was obvious, and guilt spread through her for involving him after knowing him for a mere few hours.

He must've been tired because his accent was a lot more pronounced than earlier in the evening.

And again the question whether she was all right. No, she wasn't. She was many things — scared, tired, lonely — but not all right. At that moment, all she wanted to do was curl up in her bed and sleep for as long as it took for everything to go away.

The police and their questions.

The guy with the knife.

The 'list'.

"Tiffany?"

"No," she answered at last. "I've got the police here again…"

"What's your address?"

She brushed her hand through her hair as she told Mat where she lived.

"The GPS says thirty minutes."

"That sounds about right."

He disconnected, and Tiffany looked up at Harris. "Half an hour."

He nodded. "I'll wait in the car until he arrives."

After exhaling a long breath, she said, "Thank you is not enough, but thanks anyway."

"You're very welcome." He was about to turn when he added, "I will need you to come down to the station again for a statement." And he walked away, not waiting for any reply.

****

When Mat stepped into the hall, he listened to any noises to check whether Steve and Jessica were still awake. When he spotted no light from underneath their bedroom door, he assumed they were asleep already.

Quietly, he dressed and left a note before heading out to the car, hoping his GPS lady would not lead him on another sight-seeing tour.

It took him about twenty minutes to arrive at Tiffany's. Twenty long minutes, during which he thought about was he was doing. Why he was driving to a woman's house he hardly knew. Indeed, he had enjoyed their dinner together. Underneath all her insecurities he'd found her witty and clever. He liked that. He found her attractive, not in a sexy way, but in a way that expressed her personality. Was Steve really the only reason he was helping? Did the fact that she'd been linked to the police and a dead man not ring any alarm bells?

As much as he tossed all the thoughts in his head, he kept coming back to his gut feeling that Tiffany wouldn't be Steve's friend if she were trouble. Sure, his friend was no saint, but he'd changed since he'd started going out with Jessica. Even more so, since they moved in together.

There had to be a reason he was the one she'd rung and asked for help after only knowing him for less than a day. And hopefully he was about to find out.

He parked, opened the door, but before he was able to get out someone was already standing next to him.

"Sir? I'm Sergeant Harris. May I ask for your name?"

Stunned and somewhat taken aback, Mat slowly stood, his gaze moving between the front door and the man in front of him.

"Got any identification?" Mat asked carefully.

Harris held up his badge.

"I'm Mat Apanui," Mat replied, as he retrieved his driver's license from his wallet. "A friend of Tiffany's."

The police officer glanced at the license and nodded. "Ms Cahill was in an unfortunate situation tonight where she was assaulted. She rejected the offer to stay in a safe house tonight. Will you be able to stay with her?"

Mat nodded, confused at all the information thrown at him. Unfortunate situation? Assaulted? Again, he gazed over to the door, but it was still closed. Harris must've picked up on his thought.

"I got the idea she puts up a front, but seems very scared."

Mat agreed inwardly. Yes, that'd been his impression as well.

"Thanks, Senior..." He paused, already forgotten about Harris' rank, less of disrespect, but circumstantial.

"You're welcome. And thank you for looking after her."

They shook hands before Mat lifted his hand with the car keys to lock the car.

"I'll wait until you're in the house," Harris added. "I haven't seen any movements for the last ten minutes. It wouldn't surprise me if that adrenaline rush has worn off, leaving her tired or even asleep."

With his thumb up, Mat turned and headed towards the door when his phone buzzed.

Steve.

"Mate, want to bring me up-to-date with why you're at Tiffany's? Didn't I ask you not to mess with her?"

He wasn't sure what the emotion was that raged within him. Anger at his friend for accusing him of doing something inappropriate? Confirmation that Tiffany was indeed not only a friend, but also a close friend? Worry about what he was about to find or hear?

"Okay, I've got no idea what's happening here, but Tiffany called me about half an hour ago asking for help. There was some talk about not wanting to worry you or Jessica because of a recent *situation*. So here I am. Not sure why, but I'm here. So are the police."

"Fuck."

"Let me get in and talk to her, and you'll be the first to know the details."

"Okay," Steve replied, his voice still full of concern.

"You look after your girl. I've got this one."

He disconnected the call and realised he'd missed a message. It was from Tiffany telling him about the spare keys for the door. Two minutes later, he'd found the keys and opened the door, finding Tiffany asleep on the couch. She must've felt safe enough with the police outside to give in to her exhaustion. With some relief to find her settled, he returned to the door to give the police officer another thumbs up before he closed it.

He walked along the hall to the back to find her bedroom, before seeing the stairs for the loft. Once he was upstairs, he looked for a blanket or duvet. It was a small house, but nicely furnished, old with a mix of new. The kitchen was opposite the lounge room, two small bedrooms at the other end of the house with the laundry almost hidden around the corner. He remembered Tiffany telling him that her parents had helped her buy the house to give her the chance to study.

The loft was tidy and decorated in bright colours. Too bright for him, but he knew there was always a rhyme or reason people did things, even if it was intuitively. It seemed Tiffany wanted to escape some darkness. Her mystery stirred his curiosity, and he hoped to find out more about her before he returned home in a couple of days.

He grabbed the blanket on the bed and went back to the lounge room where he placed it carefully over her. Her eyes shot open, gasping for air, and she pushed against his chest. It took her only a small moment, though, to realise it was him and that she was safe, and she calmed herself with a few deep breaths.

"Sorry," she croaked.

He touched her hands on his chest and sat next to her. "How about you lie down again?"

Despite of what had happened, and he still didn't know any particulars about it, it must've been too much for her because it didn't take her long to doze off again.

Going back to the bedroom, he grabbed a spare pillow and another blanket and tried to make himself as comfortable as possible in the single seater next to the couch. He'd had worse accommodations, especially in the huts on top of the mountains around Mt. Cook.

He'd just closed his eyes when he heard Tiffany's voice. "Thank you for coming." It was soft and just above a whisper.

"You're welcome."

"I'm surprised you came."

He opened his eyes and looked at her, but she hadn't moved and her eyes were still closed.

"Why wouldn't I?"

"You don't know me."

"That's true," he replied and closed his eyes again.

The silence around them wasn't what he was used to. He was still able to hear cars in the distance and the occasional airplane departing Melbourne airport or coming in to land. Silence outside Fox Glacier meant no noises except the whistle of the trees and the wildlife around.

Tiffany broke the stillness after a very long moment. "His name was Hudson."

He didn't reply, giving her the time she needed.

"He used to be in my classes. I thought he was a good guy. I helped him out occasionally when he lagged in his studies."

She paused, and Mat wondered whether she thought about his presence in her house after knowing her only for a few hours.

Letting out a subtle laugh, she continued. "Well, at least he was nice when I met him. After a few days of hanging out and the occasional afternoons together when I helped him with assignments, we spent a night together. The next day, I found him in his lounge room, all pale with little pearls of sweat on his forehead. I should've left then, but I was never that clever."

Mat flinched at that statement, and he swallowed, trying hard not to reply. She wasn't finished yet, with her story.

Tiffany went on. "Nothing hurts more than being rejected."

He nodded, knowing she didn't see him. Rejection wasn't something he had to encounter a lot in his life. After all, his upbringing was within a caring family, money no real issue, and women usually were happy to spend time with him. His nod had been more an acknowledgement of her words. And of her pain.

"He wanted money. I told him I didn't have any. That was when the trouble started. He got angry, throwing tantrums I'd never seen before. I made the mistake of laughing, and that was when he lashed out at me, striking me hard with his fist. I can still remember the noise of my cheekbone breaking. It was horrible. When I saw him about to swing another one, I covered my face, but he didn't stop."

His eyes shot open and his heart sank when he heard a sob. Taking a deep breath, he willed himself not to move.

"I'm okay," she assured him, as she met his gaze. How long had she been looking at him?

"I'm not sure what was worse, the pain or the realisation of how low I had sunk ending up with a drug addict. The blows were mostly aimed at my face. I wasn't able to focus. My head was dizzy and foggy. In hindsight, raising my hands to block more was out of instinct than anything else." She shrugged. "It didn't stop him, though. Another hit, and the next thing I remember, I woke up in hospital."

He closed his eyes, processing that last sentence and trying not to walk over to take her into his arms, never to let go again. It was hard to find the right words, and he wasn't sure whether his were anywhere near good enough for what she'd gone through. But he hoped. "Yet, you got up again and seem to be stronger than before."

A bubble of laughter surfaced from her, and she seemed as surprised as he was. He'd liked the sound, though.

"Stronger might be a tad exaggerated, but I'm getting there. I'm finding ground under my feet one day at a time."

He opened his eyes and studied her as she stared at the ceiling. Her short hair was a mess, her eyes puffy and red, her skin blotchy, yet he felt his stomach tighten as he recognised those imperfections were what drew him to her.

And now Hudson was dead.

Mat lounged farther back into the seat, trying to piece the puzzle together. He raked a hand through his hair, about to ask about the assault tonight, but when he saw Tiffany's eyes close and heard a soft snore, he knew he'd have to postpone his question until the morning.

He closed his eyes as well, pondering all the questions in his head. How much danger was she in?

Five

THE sun was already up when Tiffany opened her eyes the next morning. It took her a moment to figure out she was in the lounge room, but unfortunately, it didn't take long for the memories of the previous night to invade her mind. She rubbed her eyes with the balls of her hands and exhaled a long, deep breath.

Then she remembered Mat, and wriggled onto her elbows to look around. She was certain he'd arrived last night and listened to her story about Hudson. When she moved a little farther forward, she wasn't only able to smell fresh coffee, but also saw a pillow and blanket nicely stacked next to the door.

"Good morning."

She flinched.

"Apologies, I didn't mean to scare you." Mat stepped closer with two cups in his hand. "I hope you don't mind that I went through your kitchen, but I was desperate for some coffee." He held a cup towards her. "And apparently you like tea."

She raised her brows inquiringly.

"Already chatted to Steve."

A long sigh escaped her as a wave of guilt rushed through her as she thought about her decision to call Mat instead of Steve the previous night. But, in all fairness, she had done it with the best intentions.

"Just a warning, he's mad with you."

"With me?" she asked, her voice up a notch, not understanding why.

"Well, you found your voice, ay." He bit back a little chuckle as he handed her the cup of tea and sat near her feet. "He feels dumped. Not happy that you called me instead of him."

Worried, and at the same time offended because she had made the decision with the best intentions in mind, she explained, "But I don't want Jessica to worry."

His mouth curved into a smile, and his eyes lit with a gleam.

"Not sure what's so funny."

The smile spread into a grin. "Women. Jessica is fine. As soon as she heard you were assaulted, she understood. What is it between you two, anyway?"

The question surprised her. Obviously, he knew about the assault, but she couldn't remember telling him. And why did he ask about Jessica and her? "I suppose no girlfriend wants her man to have a troublemaker as a friend."

"Are you a troublemaker?"

She thought about it. Was she? No, she wasn't, but she'd been relying on Steve a lot over the last twelve months. Whenever she was scared, she'd call him. Whenever she needed advice, she'd call him. But that didn't make her a troublemaker.

"Let's say I might have overdone it a little with the aspect of the friendship."

"But isn't that what a friendship is all about? Good and bad times?"

She wagged a finger at him. "You're confusing this with a marriage."

He laughed, and the sound was wonderful to her ears.

"What did I tell you about the assault?"

"Nothing," he replied flat.

Eyebrows raised, she asked, "How do you know?"

"Senior something, something Harris."

She huffed a snort. "I thought they were bound to some confidentiality law as well."

"That was about all he told me. Like everything else, it's a piece to a big puzzle with lots of bits missing. What concerns me is that little bruise on your throat."

Instinctively, she moved her hand there.

"I didn't have the pleasure of kissing you, yet," he continued, with a smile that didn't quite reach his eyes. "So I'm damn sure it wasn't because of something I did."

"Yet?" she asked, but as soon as the word had left her lips, she regretted it. "It's from the knife," she replied in a haste, hoping to move forward from her embarrassing slipup.

His brows knitted into a frown. "What knife?"

"Okay," she said with a deep sigh. "Ehrm…When I returned…When I came home…" She exhaled another breath. "When I came home last night I had a stranger attack me, holding a knife to my throat, demanding a list."

"What list?"

She shrugged. "I have no idea."

His eyes roamed over her body, searching or appreciating, she wasn't sure, yet despite herself she blushed, aware how horrible she must look. She tried not to care, because, after all, she'd dealt with a terrifying twelve hours.

"Are you hurt anywhere else?"

She hesitated, and whispered, "My pride?"

He took a sip of his coffee and just the movement of his tongue licking his lips filled her with a rush of lust. And damn if that made her angry, because the timing couldn't have been any more wrong.

"Why your pride?" he asked, looking at his coffee as he swirled it lightly.

She shrugged again, not sure about the answer herself.

He watched her for a long moment. "You're one very mysterious lady."

Choking back a soft laugh, she replied, "Not really. I'm a lot of things, but not mysterious. Dad and I were always at each other's throats, but I was raised by loving parents who were disappointed by their daughter when she didn't follow a career after school like her brother, who's also happily married—"

"But they helped you with the house?"

She nodded. "Yes. We're kind of good now."

"Yet, I'm here and not them," he stated, looking up and holding her gaze.

Tiffany stood and walked over to the window, staring at the front yard for a long moment, scared at the brief memory of the previous night. With a big sigh, she turned to him and finally replied, "Dad will go mad when he finds out. When the police accused me of being connected with

Hudson last year, my brother wasn't very diplomatic. To say the least. I'm not sure how he'll react once he finds out about this whole mess." Letting out a soft sigh, she added, "Never mind that Melanie, his wife, was pregnant in her first couple of weeks last year. She miscarried. I don't want to be responsible for another one," she finished, just above a whisper.

"May I assume Melanie's current *situation* mirrors Jessi's?"

Tiffany rubbed her face with both hands. "Don't tell Steve that you know. He's going to kill me."

He stood as well and moved towards her. His hand touched hers, and the mere connection of their skin sent a shiver down her spine.

"Tiffany?"

"Hmm?"

"Look at me."

Slowly, she lifted her head and met his gaze.

"You're a great person. You have wit, curiosity, intellect, and you're resilient. You'll get through this," he said with a firm voice. "I know it doesn't seem like it now, but you will weather the storm and embrace the sun on the other side."

"Very poetic from someone like you."

His hand flew to his chest. "Someone like me?"

Another one of her Freudian slips. This was how she always got into trouble. "You know."

"Kiwi?"

"No!"

"Maori?"

"Oh, my God, no. Male…and…" She rolled her eyes. "And sexy."

He choked back a chuckle. "Thanks for the compliment."

"Don't let it go to your head."

"Too late."

The doorbell rang and Tiffany flinched, grabbing his arm.

"Expecting anybody?"

She was about to say no, when fear went through her like fire. "The twenty-four hours aren't over, yet."

"Twenty-four hours?"

"The deadline for giving him the list."

Mat scratched the back of his neck. "You stay here. I'll get this."

At that moment, she envied his composure and hoped it was her neighbour with her mail which had been placed in their mailbox instead of hers. The quietness in the house was eerie, with only the noise of Mat's footsteps along the hall. There were two or three seconds after the noise stopped before he opened the door.

Shit.

He was obviously not as calm as she'd expected.

And then she heard her sister-in-law's voice. "Oh! Who are you?"

"Liam, how are you, mate?" Mat replied. "You must be Melanie."

She strained to listen to their conversation, but all Tiffany was able to hear was muffled words and she wasn't able to make out what they were saying, so she was about to follow Mat to the front when Mel rushed into the room.

"Are you all right?" Her sister-in-law's high-pitched voice startled her.

"Of course I am."

"Mary from next door gave us a call saying her son heard screaming last night, and a guy was parking at the front for about an hour. What on earth happened?"

Tiffany threw herself on the couch, worried about how much could she tell her brother and Mel.

"Would you please relax? I'm fine. I didn't call you because I didn't want you to worry. You know—" She pointed at Mel's stomach.

Joining Tiffany on the couch, Mel said, "But, honey, how often have I told you, you weren't responsible for what happened last time. My body simply wasn't ready for a baby. That's all."

"How am I supposed to know whether your body still isn't ready?" Tiffany asked, without any malice but care in her voice.

The two men came into the room, both smiling, chatting away like best buddies.

Looking up at her husband, Mel asked, "And how do you two know each other?"

"Mat is Steve's old buddy from New Zealand," Liam explained.

Tiffany's gaze moved from Liam to Mat, who gave her a wink, but remained quiet.

"I've never heard you talking about a friend in New Zealand," Mel said, with a slight shrug of her shoulders.

"See, my words exactly," Tiffany piped in.

"I'm really starting to get a little complex here, guys," Mat added with a chuckle.

"Sure, I've told you about our trips to NZ." He stepped closer to his sister. "But I'd say there are more important matters on hand." He turned to Mat. "No offense."

"None taken," his friend answered with a smile.

"How about you give me a quick rundown of what happened?" Liam asked his sister.

Her chest tightened as she told him about Hudson's death and the previous night. She wasn't sure how to read his expression, but placed her hand on Mel's when she noticed her sister-in-law's pale face.

"I'm sure it's all a misunderstanding," she assured her.

Liam rubbed his hands over his face, asking Tiffany, "How safe are you here?"

With a slight lift of her shoulder, she lied, "Reasonably safe."

He cocked a brow. "Reasonably?" Gazing at his wife, the two spoke without saying a word, before he said, "Let's pack a few of your things and get you to our place for the next few days."

"I can't," Tiffany replied, somewhat louder than intended.

"Why not?" Mel asked, full of disbelief.

Tiffany stood, needing some distance. So much had happened in the last twenty-four hours, and she needed to sort things in her head. Needed to sort out some priorities.

"You're pregnant, and whether your body is or isn't ready, I'm not going to put you in any situation that might cause another miscarriage."

Mel frowned. "Honey, do you really believe me sitting at home not knowing what's happening to you isn't causing me any stress?"

Damn. Tiffany hated it when her sister-in-law was right. And damn the neighbour for calling them. And damn the whole situation. But most of all, she hoped Hudson was damned to hell. How could this all happen to her?

She'd had her life under control again. Earning money, paying off a mortgage, and treating herself to the occasional nice outfit or to the movies.

She looked from Mel, to Liam, and then to Mat, who gave her a slight nod. She wasn't sure what the nod was for, but his smile told her he was there for her.

"By the way," her brother said into the silence. "How come Mat's here? Where's Steve? Does he know?"

She hesitated, avoiding his gaze. "My guess is that Jessi's pregnant as well, but it's not official, so I wouldn't go around telling anyone."

"Pregnant?" Liam asked. "Holy fuck. The bugger hasn't even told me."

Mel shot him a glare, most likely because of his choice of words.

"He didn't really tell me either," she replied, looking at him and silently telling him, *let it go.* "The guy from last night wanted a list, but I know nothing about it. I swear. I haven't had any contact with Hudson since he gave me a fast ticket to hospital."

Liam exhaled. "We'll get it sorted, sis, but we need to get you out of here. If not our place, we need you to stay at a safe place. Somewhere they won't find you until the police gets this sorted."

"The guy last night said he saw Hudson come here, so I assume anywhere else is safe. I might go to—"

"She can come back with me. I'm sure they won't look in New Zealand for you."

Tiffany shot around and looked at him. Stunned and in disbelief.

Did he just offer for her to go to New Zealand?

"That is if you have a passport," he added, with a semi-shrug.

Her mouth was so dry from telling the story, the outraged *what?* got stuck in her throat with only a few foreign noises leaving her lips.

Going to New Zealand, she thought, as she stared at Mat, who sported a wide grin. A grin she wasn't sure how to interpret. Suddenly, even that decision seemed difficult.

With a sigh, she threw herself back onto the couch.

****

Mat looked from one stunned face to the other. He had no idea where the offer had come from, because he'd have enough work back home to keep him busy for months, especially with the new contract and his impending move to Queenstown. But he wasn't yet ready to let go of Tiffany. Wasn't ready to leave her behind without a chance to help her. He wanted to know more about her.

He wanted her. With all her flaws and her sexy smile.

Raising a brow, he watched her trying to say something, but no words were coming out of her mouth. He tried not to laugh, seeing her sit there with her mouth in the shape of an 'O'.

"Have you got a passport?" he asked into the silence.

"She can't just drop everything and hop across the water to New Zealand," Liam said.

"I agree," Mel added.

"Darling, have you got a passport?" Mat asked again.

Tiffany bobbed her head slightly in a nod. "Yes, I do. Yes, I got one last year when we planned to travel to the U.S. with Mum and Dad. Before the…you know…miscarriage." She raked a hand through her hair. "I can't afford a flight to New Zealand. And I'm not even sure whether I'm allowed to leave the country."

"You're not a suspect, are you?" Liam asked with concern.

"No. No, Senior what's-his-name told me I'm not. But that was before the guy showed up at my door, threatening me. I have to see him later on and can ask him."

"Let's do this one step after the other," Liam said, as he turned to Mat. "When are you heading home?"

"Monday morning."

"Tiff can't just fly to New Zealand with you. I mean, how long have you known her?" Mel asked.

"Okay," Liam suddenly said, raking his hand through his hair. "Let's not do anything in a rush and try to think about other alternatives. This sounds more like the last resort." He blew out a big breath. "No offense," he added, as he gave Mat a smile.

"None taken."

Mel blew out a breath as well. More than once. Mat wasn't sure whether it was to calm herself or a pregnancy thing. He looked at Liam and his grin told him not to worry about it.

"Tiffany can't just fly to New Zealand with someone she's known for…how long?" Mel asked, staring at Mat.

"Twenty-four hours," he replied nonchalantly.

Mel slanted her brows together. "Excuse me?" Then turned Liam. "No way will you allow this, will you? She can't just travel across the damn sea to be with a guy who she's known for twenty-four hours. For God's sake, it'll make me sick with worry just as much."

Mat slid his hands into his pockets as he rocked back on his heels. "I've known Steve for about twenty years."

"That can't be a good enough reason."

Tiffany stared at her, but Mat wasn't sure how to read the expression on her face. Was Mel's over-worried outburst a hormone thing, or were the two women that close?

Mat was about to say something when he noticed Tiffany wiping away a tear. He would've given anything to make this all go away for her. And, although he initially thought his idea was selfish and probably overkill, he began to think it'd be the right thing for her as well. Get away from it all and find her feet again.

And let the police do their work and solve last night's attack, as well as solve Hudson's case.

Even a week or two would do the trick and give her some distance. If during that time the police hadn't made any arrests, it'd have been at least enough time for everyone to organise an alternative living arrangement for Tiffany without too much disruption to anybody's life.

Tiffany stood, but with her shoulders slouched as if all of the world's problems were resting on them. Mat pressed the replay button in his head, wondering how he ended up in a small two-bedroom house with a woman, who wasn't necessarily model sexy, but attractive, and her brother with his wife — there'd been the nice dinner, the attack, as well as the police. All of his common sense told him to leave and run as far as possible and let them sort out the problem. Without him. His common sense told him not to touch or get involved with a woman that carried so much baggage.

But he wasn't able to.

He wasn't able to leave her, and not only because of the attraction he felt. The reason might have been the way his parents had taught him to help others. It might have been his Maori culture to fight for what he believed in, and at that moment, he believed that Tiffany needed him. Quite possibly, if Steve and Jessica weren't expecting, or Liam and Mel, it might have been a different story, but the scene in front of him was the story, and he wanted to write the happy ending.

"This is what I'm going to do," she said quietly. "Thank you for your offer, Mat. In this whole mess, I'm very grateful you were so persistent yesterday and asked me for dinner, but I cannot accept your invitation to come to New Zealand." She held her hand up when Liam was about to say something. Mat noticed a brief wordless connection pass between them. "Let me rephrase that. I would like to take a rain check."

Mat nodded and let her finish.

"I ran most of my life in one way or another, and every time I did, the mountain behind me grew bigger and wider. I'm not running again." She exhaled. "I will talk to what's-his-name Harris and stay with Mum and Dad for a while. As I mentioned before, the guy said he saw Hudson come here, so I should be safe with them. I will figure out about the damn list, and once everything is sorted, I'll go and piss on Hudson's grave. Or whatever his name is. Then, and only then, will I hit Liam for some money and find out whether New Zealand is exactly how I imagine it to be from all your stories."

The silence hung in the air like a thunderstorm, charged and ready to go. But the thunder never came. Liam gave a slow nod, and after watching her husband, so did Mel.

Disappointment trickled through Mat despite knowing she was right. And he admired her courage to face everything head on. He had to admit to himself, he was falling for her.

"Do you need a chauffeur for the day?" he asked with some hesitation.

Her smile was genuine and went right to her eyes. "I'm not sure whether I can abuse your generosity even more."

"Abuse it as much as you need to. Unfortunately, just until this afternoon, though."

She nodded. "The barbeque."

"I have another meeting tomorrow and need to return the rental around lunchtime."

"I'm happy to give you my car until you leave," Liam offered, and with his brows slightly raised, added, "Tiff might be able to return the favour and take you to her favourite fish and chip shop in St Kilda. And she has someone with her if she's in need of protection."

Mat liked the idea. His gaze went to Tiffany, and he smiled when he noticed her red cheeks. "Sounds good."

"Thanks, Liam. That'd be lovely," she said. "Except the protection part."

"Just in case. I will take this beauty—" He nodded towards Mel. "—to morning tea and will see you tomorrow to pick up the car."

"You're not coming to Steve's barbeque?" Tiffany asked.

"Nope." And, with a roll of his eyes, he added, "We've got tickets to see a musical."

"Got into trouble again?" Tiffany asked with a snort.

Another eye roll.

Tiffany laughed. "Have fun." And she turned to Mat and explained. "Liam looooves musicals. It wouldn't surprise me if he'd forgotten their anniversary again."

Mel stood as well, stepped next to her sister-in-law, and placed a kiss on her cheek. "It was the doctor's appointment. You look after yourself and keep us informed with every little detail, okay?"

"Will do."

It surprised Mat when Mel came to him. He noticed her hesitation, but then she took his necklace in her hand. "A man who wears his heritage with pride." Meeting his gaze, she said, "Please look after her. Tiff and I aren't blood related, but she's as close to a sister as one could have. Steve and Liam trust you, so I will, too."

"Tiffany trusts me as well," he said with a faint voice.

She shook her head. "She believes in you. You're one lucky man, so don't muck it up."

As he wasn't sure how to respond, he simply nodded. *She believes in you.* Trust. Believe. He wasn't sure about the difference, but apparently, there was a big one to Mel.

Tiffany took the couple to the door, and Mat heard another few mumbled words before the sound of the front door followed by the noise of her footsteps that told him they were alone again.

A few minutes later, she stood in front of him, hands on hips. "I have no idea how our stars aligned, but I'm super grateful for it. So let's tackle this problem."

It took him only a few long strides until he stood in front of her. On impulse, he leaned in and brushed his lips gently against hers, before he fully claimed them. Soft at first, tasting the remnants of the tea. He pulled her closer, deepening the kiss at the same time. She opened up for him, and for a wonderful moment, their tongues touched. He hadn't felt so much in a simple kiss for a long time, but slowly pulled back.

"Sorry," he whispered.

Her eyes flew open.

"I needed to know what these lips feel like," he said, as he traced her bottom lip with his thumb.

She gave him a shy smile. "Did they pass the test?"

"And more. But before I lose complete control over my body, how about we get back to your plan?"

Tilting her head towards his face, she kissed him again, and he slid his hand around her waist, drawing her in close again. Her hands drifted up his chest, melting his insides as he held back a groan at the feel of her fingertips skimming over his body. Relishing the feel of his hands at her waist now, he used his thumbs to gently caress her skin beneath her belly button. The feel and the taste of her woke all his senses, and he was surprised by the craving in his body.

When she broke the kiss, a smile tugged at her lips. "I needed to be certain as well."

He laughed as he gently pulled her into an embrace. "Glad we got this sorted."

He pulled her in even closer in a hug, placing a light kiss on her forehead. "And we'll get everything else sorted as well. Ka mate te kāinga tahi, ka ora te kāinga rua [4]."

---

[4] When one house dies, a second lives.

Historically used when two houses or families are merged due to the unfortunate circumstances of one particular family. However, this could be used when something good emerges from misfortune.

Six

WITHIN the next twenty-four hours, Tiffany was sitting in front of Sergeant Harris and Senior Constable Jones at the police station for the second time. She glanced warily around the interview room, nauseous with apprehension. It was furnished simply and coldly, with white walls and nothing but a table and a few chairs. Unlike in most of the movies, this room had a small window front. *Déjà vu,* she thought. Yet, this time it was Mat sitting next to her instead of Steve.

Harris introduced Mat to Jones before he asked, "What brings you to Melbourne?"

"Business."

"What kind of business? Personal curiosity."

"I'm hoping to expand my company with the help of a travel company from Melbourne."

Harris didn't break eye contact with Mat and seemed genuinely interested. "What's the nature of your company?"

"I own a helicopter tour company in Fox Glacier."

Tiffany noticed Senior Constable Jones was hanging onto Mat's every word. Not only that, she'd studied him intently as well. It didn't surprise her, because, after all, he looked sexy as hell, and she still had to pinch herself that he was sitting right next to her, instead of enjoying his time in Melbourne. More so, she had to pinch herself that he'd kissed her. And what a kiss it'd been. She watched him as he politely satisfied Harris' curiosity. Everything inside her was on full alert as she looked at him in the loose-fitting black cargo pants and his black T-shirt, which, again, only revealed part of his tattoo.

"Miss Cahill?"

Sergeant Harris' voice hauled her back from her thoughts, and she hoped he didn't notice the flushed cheeks that had resulted from her images of Mat.

"Sorry."

The twitching lines of his mouth told her he was trying hard to hold back a smile.

"This is a written statement of what you told me yesterday. Could you please read through it and sign to acknowledge the accuracy of the events?"

Tiffany took a deep breath, preparing herself to revisit the terrifying moments of the previous night again. She read the first few lines, but had to start over, her mind not wanting to take in the words. Forcing her not to go back to the five minutes again that had scared her so much.

Her will was stronger, though, and a few minutes later, she asked for a pen to place her signature at the bottom.

Harris took the piece of paper and moved it to Jones who placed it into a file.

"We'll give you a copy before you leave today."

Tiffany nodded, and when she was about to stand, Mat said, "Sir, I'm not sure whether it's of any relevance, but Tiffany's brother came this morning after he'd been called by a neighbour…"

Harris first looked at Jones, who took a piece of paper and a pen before starting to take notes.

Tiffany stared at Mat, surprised at his statement, but nonetheless grateful. "After last year's episode with the police taking me to the station, my brother asked my neighbour if he could leave his number with them. We've become good neighbourly friends since," she explained.

"The son had heard someone screaming and saw a guy parking at the front door for about an hour. When he'd told his mother, she, in turn, rang Liam. Perhaps he, as in the son, might be able to help. The guy in the car for an hour could've been you or the other guy."

Harris nodded thoughtfully. "I appreciate that. Do you have a name?"

"Mary Crawley. Her son's name is Leo."

"How old is Leo?" Jones asked.

Tiffany shrugged. "Late teens I'd say, but I'm honestly not sure."

Jones made more notes, and Harris asked, "Anything else?"

Tiffany wracked her brain, but nothing came to mind. She closed her eyes, forcing herself back into the situation, trying hard to return to the moment. "He had dark olive skin, at least that's what his hand looked like. Terrible body odour, which wasn't the smell of sweat, but a bit like urine. I remember I was embarrassed thinking I peed myself, which I hadn't."

When she felt Mat's hand on her back, moving up and down, she opened her eyes and looked straight into Harris' gaze.

"That could be very useful," he said.

She wasn't sure, whether it was simply a platitude or if he meant it. Either way, she was glad she was able to contribute something as well.

Jones stood and left the room. Harris said, "She'll get you a copy of that statement."

Tiffany nodded.

"Thomas Terrill lived under the name Hudson Ford and imported drugs from South America under a third name. Insiders have told us he wanted out. We gather, but we're not sure, that the list you were asked for is a list of dealers he worked with."

"In the movies they get such a list first before they kill," Tiffany stated, with some surprise to the latest development.

His subtle chuckle sounded genuine. "I agree. But this is not a movie. Do you know anything about this list?"

"No. As I told you, the last time I saw him was over twelve months ago when he hit me straight into hospital. I thought he was a user, nothing more."

"We spent about two hours this morning turning Tiffany's house up-side-down to find the list, but came up with nothing," Mat explained. "It's hard because we weren't sure what to look for."

Harris nodded. "Any trace of a break in?"

She shook her head.

"We've spread the word there's a list from Thomas in the hands of the police."

Her eyes narrowed. "Excuse me? You've spread the word?"

A little smile appeared on his face. "Some bits from the movies aren't as far-fetched as they seem.

We're hoping to divert the interest from you. But we still need you to be at a safe place."

The police comparing her current situation with a movie didn't sit well with Tiffany. After all, it wasn't a movie but her life. And a dead person had put her into this movie-like situation. She burst into a round of curses and dire threats of what she would've done to him if he hadn't been dead and ignored everyone's stare at the same time.

She thought about the list. A list with drug dealers. A list with names. Or addresses. A list…But she came up with a blank. Nothing had been in the mail. No email. No messages. She wasn't able to remember a list.

"Miss Cahill?"

"I've packed some stuff and will stay with my parents for a few days." For good measure, she added, "Or as long as it takes."

"Here in Melbourne?"

"Yes. I've thought about it long and hard. They, whoever they are, shouldn't know their address, because Hudson never knew."

Jones came back in and handed her a piece of paper. The copy of the statement. She thanked her.

"Will you stay with her?" Harris asked, as he looked at Mat.

He shook his head. "I'm heading back to NZ on Monday. I'm not able to extend my stay as much as I would like to."

Harris responded with a nod.

The next ten minutes, they discussed the police's plans to approach the case, as well as noting down more of Tiffany's information, like her parents' address.

Once she was out of the building half an hour later, she took Mat's hand and said, "Will you join me for some fish and chips in St. Kilda?"

"I'd love to," he replied with a big grin.

Once they were in the car, she directed him through Melbourne to the other side of the city.

"I like your voice much better than the GPS lady," he said as he pointed to his navigation system.

She let out a soft snort. "Thank you for the compliment. Can't say that anybody's said that to me before."

His laugh went right through her and pooled in her groin. The extent of comfort and attraction surprised her, considering she'd known him for a bit over a day. After Hudson had beaten her unconscious, and she'd ended up in hospital, she'd withdrawn from life for a few months, deferring some of her classes, but going to the pub where she'd worked behind the bar. Guarded and cautious around others, she hated feeling vulnerable. She had begun to build a defensive wall around her heart.

But her wall wasn't tall enough when it came to Mat. He'd pulled down her defences with ease in such a short time.

She turned towards him and placed her hand on his arm. The simple touch brought every nerve in her body alive, the bombardment of sensations for a brief moment causing her head to spin. With an effort, she said just above a whisper, "Thank you."

He cocked a brow. "It's not really that much of a compliment comparing you to a GPS voice, but—"

"I meant for everything else. For being here. For calling yesterday and making sure I was okay. For caring."

Mat glanced at her before he took her hand in his. "You're very welcome."

"I'm relieved Hudson is dead," she said with an exhale. "I know it's not a nice thing to say...nice is not the correct word...it's inappropriate, but when I had the police at my doorstep last year it was because he'd told them I'd given him the drugs. They'd arrested him on drug charges. The bastard blamed it all on me. I suppose in a way it was good I'd ended up in hospital, at least we had the medical records to prove he'd beaten me up."

"How did they prove it was him?"

"At least he had the decency to drop me off at the hospital. They have cameras at the emergency entrance."

"Good thinking," he commented with a nod.

They drove in silence for a while, Tiffany engulfed in trying to forget about that terrible day. Did she have the right to be relieved that someone else was dead? Shaking the thought out of her mind, she focussed back on the road.

"Turn right over there and find a park. Let's introduce you to the best fish and chips in Australia."

Mat chuckled. "Can't wait."

But before she was able to open the door, he gently pulled her back towards him. He studied her eyes for a moment before he reached across, laced his fingers through her hair, and cupped the back of her neck softly to pull her closer. Everything inside her stilled when he traced the curve of her lips with his tongue, sending a shiver down her spine. The touch of his lips against hers was so soft, so light and, yet, it had all her nerves on alert. He moved his other hand up her arm and cupped her face, before he kissed her lightly, albeit with a hint of fire that left her breathless.

When he broke away, he dropped his forehead to hers and whispered, "I'm sorry you have to go through all this."

Tiffany licked her lips to savour his taste when she tilted her head. "Some things are meant to be, Grandma always said."

A corner of his mouth curved. "She sounds like an intelligent woman."

She nodded with a smile, remembering her grandma with fondness. "Yes, she was," she agreed. "A wealth of wisdom."

****

They got out of the car and strolled along the beach to the food outlets. Mat looked around, enjoying the sound of the waves along the foreshore and the warm breeze carrying the scent of the salt water. He shook his head in amusement at the noisy seagulls, eager to snatch a chip or two from the small children.

Tiffany hauled him back from his thoughts. "So, how do you know my brother, Liam?"

"Spent some nasty days with him and Steve at Dad's beach house east of Auckland."

She turned to look at him. "Nasty?"

"Boys' stuff," he replied with a crooked grin.

"Not sure I want to know more."

"Let's just say we weren't angels, and Dad was always pissed off by the mess we left."

"Not anymore, though?" Tiffany asked with a soft chuckle.

A soft sigh escaped him as he remembered those days when the three of them were stuck in the beach house for a week with no idea how to cook. So, it was fast food and lots of beer, and equally lots of girls — the older Steve and Liam became, the less alcohol and girls were involved. It'd still been some fun days.

"Steve has been over occasionally, but the business has kept me busy, so it was always a quick trip to Queenstown."

"So you're a party boy?"

"Nah. Not sure when it happened, but I've grown up. Probably when I started my business." He lifted his shoulder in a shrug. "Fair enough, Dad helped me with some money to start it, but I've paid it back and have been solid since."

They bought their lunch at a small fish and chip shop and returned to the beach where they sat at a small picnic table along the foreshore. Tiffany had been right, the fish and the chips were indeed delicious.

"What about you? Are you a party girl?" he asked, as he opened the bottle of cola.

She contemplated the question. "Used to be. Got myself into trouble from week to week and blamed Mum and Dad for my misfortunes."

"How come?"

"Liam has always been the charmer with the intelligence. Everything came easy to him. Dad was the one who always blamed me for making the wrong decisions. Thinking back, I don't think they *were* wrong, but when he'd say go left, I went right, without giving it any second thought."

He looked up to meet her gaze, but found her staring into the distance. It didn't sound like the easiest upbringing, but he'd learnt early in his life his childhood hadn't been the norm. He wouldn't claim it to have been perfect. Yes, they'd had money, but there was the constant group of reporters, or the fake friendships because his father was famous, the girls who thought he was rich and were absolutely disappointed when he wasn't able to afford to take them out to the movies — he'd preferred to spend his pocket money on magazines or CDs.

"I suppose you figured to think about it before you turn left or right, at last?"

A smile lingered on her face as their gazes met. "Yes," she replied with an exhale. "It feels good. It's tough, but when I can't keep my eyes open on a Friday night because I'm dead tired on my feet, I remind myself I have a lovely house I live in, some savings in the bank, and soon I'll have finished my studies and be able to start my own business." She paused. "That's the plan anyway."

Mat took a chip and dipped it into the tomato sauce. "I like a woman with a plan."

She looked back into the distance again, the smile on her face gone, replaced by something like wistfulness.

Reaching out, he took her hand in his. "A penny for your thoughts."

"Nothing," she said, with a shake of her head, yet too quickly.

"C'mon. You've been so good opening up to me."

Studying her face, he thought he saw a little blush on her cheeks.

"Life's all about timing and fate, isn't it? Mine sucks."

He frowned. "How come?"

"I meet you while I have the police breathing up my neck, but you're also from a different country."

"Queenstown is closer than Cairns, you realise that, don't you?"

"Is it?" she asked, with her brows raised.

He nodded with a grin.

Her expression changed to sadness. "Shows my lack of education, I suppose."

"No, not at all. Shows that geography is not your strength. We all have things we're good at, but no one is good at everything." He gulped down the last of his drink, then said, "How about we get you to your parents so you can get ready for the barbeque tonight."

She checked the time. "Yes, good idea."

They disposed of the rubbish, and with his hand on her lower back, he walked her to the car. He would've loved to stay much longer, talk to her a little more to find out who she was, what she liked, but at the same time, he knew she would need some time this afternoon to settle in her parents' house.

And to explain the happenings of the last twenty-four hours, including someone threatening her life. Not to mention that the reason for the temporary move was the danger she could be in.

****

When Tiffany woke the next morning, it took her a moment again to remember she was back at her parents' house, in her old bedroom. The walls were still painted in dark pink, although the colour had faded, and the door to her walk-in-robe was still replaced by a beaded door curtain with lots of small butterflies. Over in the other corner of the room was the old child desk with a few of her books she'd loved reading.

For the first time in all those years, she was actually able to smile and feel comfortable with the memories. It hadn't been a bad childhood. She knew her parents loved her and had given her all the opportunities they'd been able to, yet her father's and her own characters had not been compatible. They'd clashed often. But now that she was thinking about it, she always had one friend or another, or a boyfriend, she'd shared good times with. Coming home wasn't high on the list on her favourite memories, but there'd been the occasional moments when all four of them had enjoyed a laugh while watching a movie, a laugh while listening to each other's stories, or a little cry about another relationship gone wrong. Holidays hadn't been that bad, either. Why did it always take her so long to see the good things in life?

Was it Mat? Was it his company that made her feel so invincible at the moment?

She touched her lips and remembered their kiss last night when he'd dropped her off after the barbeque.

It'd been a wonderful evening, with lots of funny stories about Steve and Mat — some hilarious, some a little close to *too much information*, some honest and at the edge of sad. She hadn't wanted the evening to end, feeling like a teenager being dropped off at her parents' house. But he'd understood. He always understood and always saw the good side in things.

And despite the twenty-four-hour deadline, she hadn't heard from her attacker. She hoped the reason was he didn't know her location.

After a long stretch, she grabbed her phone and checked it for messages.

Got Liam's car. Will pick you up at 10 to take you to Torquay.

This simple message gave her a shiver of excitement, put a smile on her face, and had her body shuddering in anticipation. She stretched again and reached for the curtains. Sunshine. It was going to be one wonderful day.

It took Tiffany half an hour to get organised. Not that she'd packed for the beach before she'd come back to her childhood home, but she'd found an old bikini and a nice beach towel. That should do the trick for the day.

"Good morning, darling," her mother greeted her as she came into the kitchen. "You're up early."

"Steve's friend will take me to Torquay."

"The same friend who kept you in the car for at least fifteen minutes last night?"

Tiffany blushed. "Sorry, I hope we didn't wake you."

Shaking her head, her mother replied with a little smile, "Not at all. It's nice to see you happy. It suits you. Will you tell me about that new man? I take it he's nice, considering he's Steve's friend."

Tiffany sat, exhaling a big sigh. "Yes, but he's from New Zealand."

Her mother, Lesley, was in her late-fifties, but life had been good to her, and it showed. Tiffany admitted that as much as she and her father would log heads on many things, he loved his wife, and vice versa.

"Where's Dad?"

"Down the street grabbing his beloved Sunday paper."

Tiffany choked back a chuckle. How could she forget? He'd done it all her life and possibly even longer.

"He had a little talk with Liam last night. Your explanation about having some painting done didn't sound right to him."

Tiffany stood and switched on the kettle before she got a cup and a tea bag.

"Oh darling, why didn't you tell us?"

"Is Dad angry?" she asked without looking at her mother.

"No, not at all. He's proud of you that you made the decision to come home."

"Proud?"

"Darling, he's not stupid. He knows you two have your differences. It must've taken a lot of convincing to make you come here."

The whistle of the kettle interrupted their conversation. She poured the water in the cup and added some sugar. Her mother's comment about Tiffany's pride and her father not being angry surprised her, and she pondered that for a moment. Her relationship with her father wasn't perfect, but since her stay in the hospital, they were able to talk to each other without ending up in a fight. Even stay in the same house without blaming each other for some irrelevant issue from the past.

And she started to enjoy their new relationship.

She placed her cup on the table and sat. Her mother touched her hand. "It's not out of this world. Just divided by a little bit of water. And come to think of it, I believe it's closer than Darwin."

Tucking a strand of hair behind her ear, Tiffany said, "I really sucked at school. Everyone seems to know except me."

Lesley touched Tiffany's nose with the tip of her finger. "You knew that, too, but you're probably still scared to think about tomorrow."

Tiffany took her mother's hand in hers. "I'm scared, Mum. I'm scared to give in to my feelings and have to pick myself up again."

"That's the circle of life. You live and you learn. Is he nice?"

And there was that rush through her body again. The one that had every single nerve on alert. The rush which pooled in the pit of her stomach. The rush which reminded her of that kiss last night, a kiss like she'd never been kissed before.

Tiffany didn't reply, but smiled at her mother.

"I take that as a yes."

"Is that how it feels when meet someone you could love?"

Again, the sound of her mother's beautiful laughter she enjoyed hearing so much.

"Yes," was all her mother said. A simple *Yes* that said so much more though. A *Yes* that said, *When you meet the right man, you know.* And it said, *Yes* as in, *It makes you feel just this way.*

"Mat has invited me to visit him in New Zealand."

Lesley looked up with another one of those beautiful smiles. "Oh darling, this is a wonderful opportunity."

She nodded. "Yes, it is," she whispered. "But I want to go over there and enjoy it. I need this whole business about Hudson done and sorted."

"Even in his death he's a pain, that awful man."

Tiffany exhaled a soft laugh at her mother's words. They weren't words she was used to from her. All her teenage life it was all about manners, language, and etiquette. Hearing her mother talking so close to degrading about someone surprised her. Hudson's actions with her ending up in hospital had shaken her mother in particular. She'd fussed about Tiffany for weeks, close to worrying herself sick.

"Yes, he was, and as awful as it sounds, I'm glad he's dead. Makes me just as awful, I suppose."

"No, it doesn't."

Tiffany shot around at the sound of her father's deep voice. "Good morning, Dad."

He sat next to her with a big sigh. "It's not nice to eavesdrop, and I apologise."

She dropped her head, partly ashamed, partly worried about another confrontation, but mostly trying to recall what had been said. Exhaling a long breath, she closed her eyes, about to say something, when her father beat her to it.

"We're happy to pay for the airfare," he said, as he placed his hand on her shoulder.

"Tim, that is a wonderful idea," her mother said.

"Dad—"

"You deserve a little holiday. You've been working hard the last few years."

Left speechless by the surprise, she lifted her head and met her father's gaze. It'd been a long time since she'd seen him smile at her. A genuine smile coming from his heart. Warmth rushed through her and for the first time she was able to remember, he'd said go left and she wanted to go left, too.

"This is very kind of you, Dad, but how about I take one step after the other."

Leaning back, Tim gave a slow nod. "So, this terrible man is dead, but left you a list?"

She nodded, not surprised her father not only knew all about what had happened, but also knew details. Her brother was nothing if not very thorough.

"And you haven't got a clue about any list?" her mother asked.

Tiffany snorted. "What is this? Playing Jessica Fletcher and Sherriff Tupper?"

With a shrug, her mother replied, "It always worked for them."

"Mum, this is not television. I don't know anything about a list, and to be totally honest, I don't want to know anything about a list. It's scary. The police think they killed Hudson for the list. God only knows what they're capable of."

Her father rubbed his hand over his face. "We're not pretending to be anything, but because of exactly that, Hudson's death, we shouldn't ignore the situation, but try to get it solved as soon as possible. I have no intention of visiting you in hospital again."

"Now you're scaring me." Lesley gave a little exaggerated shiver. "You might want to go to New Zealand sooner rather than later. Talking about the neighbours from across the sea, aren't you expecting him sometime soon?"

"Shoot," Tiffany exclaimed as she stood in a rush. "I'd better get ready." She kissed her mother on the cheek. "So loved the conversation, Mum, but I've gotta run."

"Will you be safe?" her mother asked.

She bit her lip for a long moment. "I keep telling myself they only know where I live and nothing else. The twenty-four-hour deadline is over and nothing's happened yet. I don't want to hide away, and honestly, I feel safe with Mat."

"Be safe anyway," her mum pleaded.

"I will, Mum. I promise."

She was about to leave when she froze for a second before she turned to her father. Not sure whether left or right was the way to go, she hesitated before leaning in to place a kiss on his cheek as well. "Thank you, Dad."

He took her hand. "We'll get through this, Tiffany. I promise. And as much as I understand your reasoning, I agree with your mum, please stay safe."

She blinked a couple of times to hold back the tears, but a few escaped nonetheless. Initially, she thought it'd been his promise, but once she stepped back into her old room, she realised it'd been something he'd said. Something so small, but meaning the world to her.

We.

We'll get through this.

Seven

TIFFANY'S first thought on Monday morning was Mat, and her lips curled into a smile.

Her second thought was the infamous list, and that she still hadn't heard from anybody.

To her relief.

But she didn't want to think about that now, because she had only a few more hours left with Mat and, damn, if she didn't want to make the most of it. She needed to ignore the list problem for a little longer.

The fact she had known Mat for only a couple of days didn't do anything to her emotional state. It took a lot of effort on her part to keep her composure, especially as her heart simply didn't want to slow down. Her whole body responded to her misery of having to say goodbye to her new friend who happened to live in another country.

Whether closer than some Australian cities or not, it didn't matter to her.

She'd offered to take him to the airport, so she was able to return Liam's car later on, but the main reason was, of course, that she wanted to spend another few hours with him. Wanted to listen to his sexy Kiwi accent a little longer. Wanted to spend more time with the man who made her laugh and feel important. Never in her whole life would she have thought someone could have such an effect on her like this. Especially not after her experience with Hudson — may he *not* rest in peace.

She'd taken Mat for a drive along the Great Ocean Road the previous day, which they'd both fully enjoyed. The conversation had been wide spread from family to relationships and business to the beautiful places in both countries. Mat was well-travelled around the world, and she envied him for it. Yet, the more he talked about his business and New Zealand, the more she wanted to visit him. Risky or not so risky. In her heart, she believed she was able to trust him. As did Steve. And Liam didn't have a bad word to say about him, either, except that he didn't know anything about Australian football. Something Tiffany was able to live with.

And now she had to say goodbye to him already. After two and a bit days. They walked side-by-side towards the entrance through to customs. The airport was busy, and noisy, with people coming and going in different directions.

Exhaling a long breath, she looked up at him, and it seemed he struggled as well.

Was that wishful thinking?

"This is it, baby."

Hearing the endearment turned her legs into jelly, and all she was able to do was give a simple nod.

He brought his free hand to the side of her face, cupping her cheek, and touched her mouth with his. Tiffany closed her eyes, absorbing the feeling with every cell in her body so she would be able to remember it for as long as it'd take her to see him again. When he broke the kiss and wiped a tear from her cheek with his thumb, she noticed she'd lost the fight to hold them back.

"Hey, baby, don't, please. I'll give you a call when I get home, ay."

Again, she barely nodded.

"And we can chat online."

She wiped her face with her hands, knowing that'd be short-lived because of the limited download she had available each month. Yet, she smiled and nodded, not knowing how else to respond.

He leaned in to touch her lips with his again, and she kissed him back with everything she had. Everything she wasn't able to express with words. Her feelings for him, the sadness inside her to have to let go already, the joy he'd given her the last few days, and the contentment for knowing him. Not ready yet for him to ease away, she placed her hand on his chest, letting the heat spread through her as well.

"Taku whaiāipo.[5]"

Again, she had no idea what he'd said, but it sounded incredibly sweet and sexy. She rolled her eyes at herself at the ridiculous notion that something unknown sounded sexy.

What if he'd called her an ugly cow?

She let out a little snort to which he responded with a cocked brow.

"I'm sorry. I'm utterly ridiculous, most likely to help me through this situation, but I'm sincerely hoping you didn't call me an ugly cow. It sounded beautiful and so...so..."

"My sweetheart."

Biting her lip, she tilted her head and studied him for a moment. "I like it," she whispered.

"You'd better get used to it."

---

[5] My sweetheart.

Then he turned, the sliding doors in front of them opened, and he disappeared behind them.

Just like that.

And just like that, she noticed how much she'd fallen for him. Fallen for his charm. There was no way it was a simple crush.

She'd made sure men weren't on her menu any more. She'd given up on them and the philosophy had worked well the last twelve months. Nobody had interested her in the slightest.

Then Mat had come along. This tall, well-tanned, short-haired, tattooed man, with dark chocolate brown eyes, who wore a necklace, spoke with the sexiest accent she'd ever heard, and stole her heart.

Just like that.

She touched her finger to her mouth, remembering the feel of his lips and the sound of his voice.

When she got bumped by a group of passengers with their trolleys, she startled. Looking around, a slight embarrassment rushed through her, and she spun around and walked back to the car, her thoughts still with Mat.

Suddenly, she knew she couldn't care less about Hudson and his list and was determined to follow Mat as soon as possible.

She was no suspect, but a victim.

She was a holder of a passport, and if Queenstown was closer than Darwin or Cairns, she was hoping the fares would be closer to her budget as well. Or take up on her parents' offer to help her out.

Shaking her head, she smiled at the thought that suddenly her budget was non-existent as well as her pride. The need to see him again was bigger and more important than any of her plans she'd had and followed over the last few months. And Duncan from the pub would happily give her some time off, too. She deserved the break.

Starting the engine, she smiled, happy with her new plan.

The drive back into Melbourne was tedious and long because of the morning traffic. It took her more than an hour and a half to get to Liam's house to drop off the car.

"Want to come in for a cuppa?" Mel asked her as she entered the house to hand over the keys.

"You're not working today?"

"I've got the next couple of days off to try to relax and get my blood pressure under control."

Guilt shot through Tiffany. "Cos of me?"

"Nah. We're simply over-cautious about it, that's all. It's been a hectic week at work."

Still feeling responsible, there were no words to express how much guilt she carried. Despite knowing it wasn't anywhere near enough, she whispered, "I'm so sorry."

Mel waved her hand. "Let's have a cup of lemon tea with some ginger. That's supposed to be calming." And, as she tucked a strand of Tiffany's hair behind her ear, she added, "And it seems you're in need of some calming as well."

Tiffany choked back a snort. "That obvious?"

Her sister-in-law smiled. "And some more."

"What have I done, Mel?"

She looped her arm through Tiffany's. "I have a feeling Cupid's been for a visit. Let's get this tea done. I want to hear all about it."

"Only if I can have a normal black tea."

"I'm afraid we don't have normal tea in the house."

Tiffany stopped. "Liam okay with that?"

"Nope, but at the moment he does about anything to keep his wife happy," Mel replied, the twinkle in her eyes telling Tiffany just how much she was enjoying it.

"You're naughty."

Her sister-in-law laughed. "Don't tell anybody."

They made their way to the kitchen. Tiffany had long given up on feeling jealous or envious about her brother and his wife living in such a beautiful house. It was a small house considering the amount of money Liam earned as a business man, yet it still looked luxurious to Tiffany. He'd bought the house soon after signing his first contract with his international company. It was modest then. But, as to use her mother's words, it had charm and character. They'd added a barbeque area, and it wouldn't surprise Tiffany if the first swing sets had been ordered already. Liam's excitement about the pregnancy was obvious in many ways. It must've been a nightmare for him to keep silent about it until the pregnancy was declared safe.

Warmth spread inside her. He was going to be such a great dad.

They stepped into the kitchen. Tiffany loved the rustic look with all the modern conveniences.

"Tell me about Mat," Tiffany said as she sat, watching her sister-in-law opening one cupboard door after the other until she had cups, tea, and sugar.

Mel tilted her head with a shrug. "And I was about to ask you the same question."

"C'mon, Mel, as soon as you found out that Liam knows him you were dying to get all the information."

With a little flick of the finger, she turned on the kettle before joining Tiffany at the table. "You know I'm really glad I've got a sister-in-law like you. I like it that we're able to sit down and talk like this."

Tiffany choked back a chuckle. "It's been quite a year, I suppose. I've come a long way and appreciate the people around me nowadays."

Mel nodded. "I know. Awful, though, that you had to go through this first."

She shrugged. "Better late than never, I suppose."

"Anyway," her sister-in-law piped up, most likely to not let the mood turn too depressing. "Of course, I asked Liam about Mat. You know how nosy I am. *And* protective." She leaned back into the chair. "Liam had only good things to say about Mat. Oh, except his dad used to be an All Black. You know the boys, especially with the kiwis winning the World Cup. That doesn't sit well with any of them." She shrugged. "Dad's rich, but Mat always took the hard way, wanting to prove he could do it on his own. I think he spent quite a few months with a Maori tribe to learn about that part of his history, before studying to be a Phys Ed teacher."

"I didn't know any of this," Tiffany admitted.

"Honey, once you meet someone, you don't tell them your life's story on your first date."

"True," she replied. "He mostly told me about where he works and what he does."

"Because that's what he loves. People tend to talk about what they like. You do it. All I've heard the last few months is about legalities in business, debits and credits, and God knows what," she finished with a laugh. Mel stood when the kettle whistled. "I'd say all you will hear from me over the next few months is an encyclopaedia worth of pregnancy details."

"Lord, have mercy on me," Tiffany replied with a laugh.

Taking the cup of tea from her sister-in-law, she sniffed the steam and crinkled her nose at the aroma. "Are you sure about the calming effect?"

"Oh, you're such a wuss, just like your brother. Try it. It tastes good, especially if you add a little bit of sugar."

She pulled the sugar bowl closer, took a teaspoon, and added some more of the sweetener...one teaspoon and then another. Hesitating, she looked at her sister-in-law who shook her head, although with a smile on her face, and decided two was enough.

"So, what are you going to do now?"

Tiffany stirred the sugar into the tea. "Dad will take me to the police station this afternoon. I want to clarify a few things, and I suppose Dad wants to chat to Harris as well." A trace of a smile played across her lips as she lifted the cup. "I have a feeling he worries and would like to have the full story from the police."

"Of course he worries, Tiff," Mel said, as she placed her hand on Tiffany's. "I know your relationship with him was never the best, but it's improving, and in his awkward way, he wants to show you he's there for you."

Taking a sip of the tea and trying hard not to show her dislike of the taste, she finally replied, "I know. And, you know, it feels nice. Not only being at Mum and Dad's, but also to be able to talk things through. I feel safe, I suppose."

"Talking about safe. Liam said he talked to you last night and mentioned there was no news regarding the attacker."

A little shiver ran down Tiffany's spine when reminded about the assault. "It feels surreal. I'm staying away from the house because I'm too scared that's the only place this guy knows I could be, but even a couple of drive bys by the police didn't result in anything." She placed the cup on the table. "I'm starting to think they've found the damn list and forgotten about me."

"Don't get too complacent, though," Mel cautioned.

She shook her head and huffed out a snort. "Now that Mat's returned to New Zealand I will really have to get my head around it and get it sorted. I'm glad Dad's coming with me to see the police."

"You know we're here for you, too. And so is Steve."

A smile tugged at her lips. "Thank you."

"So," Mel exclaimed, as she slid her slippers off her feet and propped her legs on the chair next to her. "Tell me more about Mat."

Trying to keep an expressionless face was much harder when it came to this new man in her life, and that smile she'd been wearing for the last few days was back again. "Dad must've talked to Liam and then offered to help me financially to visit him in New Zealand. If the police give me a clearance to go, I probably will. It'd be perfect timing with my studies and such." She expelled a sigh. "It's scary, though, to trust a man again. Especially when there's going to be so much water between me and my family."

"Oh, honey. From what I hear, you don't have to worry about that. And from what I also hear, your dad would not let you go if he had any doubts what-so-ever."

Tiffany smiled at her sister-in-law's statement. It was true that if her father had any doubts, or even Liam, they wouldn't let her leave.

Mel placed a hand on Tiffany's. "New Zealand is stunning—"

"Have you been there?" Tiffany interrupted her.

She wrapped her hands around the teacup. "No, but I watch all the travel shows, hoping that one day Liam will have enough time off to explore the world with us."

Tiffany chuckled. "Good luck with that."

"It's a beautiful place. And if it doesn't work out, you'll grab a rental car and explore the island on your own."

On your own. The words struck her. She was good at being on her own. She liked being able to make her own plans. To come and go as she pleased. And what if it didn't work out with Mat? What if he discovered she wasn't at all what he wanted? She'd still have the time of her life exploring New Zealand.

"My new motto is to think positive, though. It's going to work out, and it's going to be wonderful," she said with more conviction than she felt, because being in New Zealand on her own wasn't what she had in mind. She wanted to be with Mat.

Tiffany finished the last little bit of her herbal tea that, in the end, didn't taste as bad as she'd initially thought, and stood. "I think I'd better get going. I still have to catch the bus back to Mum and Dad's."

"Would you like me to give you a lift?" her sister-in-law asked.

Tiffany appreciated the offer, but there was no way she would, even though unintentional, put Mel into danger, and replied, "No, thank you. I'm fine. It's one changeover between busses, and I enjoy the time on a bus at this time of the day. It gives me time to think and time to read a little bit of my books on the tablet as well."

Mel stood, too, and took the empty cups to the sink before she turned to Tiffany. "I don't want to worry you or be over cautious here, but please do take care. I wouldn't like anything to happen to you. It seems like these people are dangerous."

A sizzle of undefined emotions rushed over Tiffany, and she wasn't sure whether it was fear, worry, or the appreciation of her pregnant sister-in-law's concern. Which in return worried her so much, hoping it wouldn't put the pregnancy at risk.

Of course, she had thought about the idea that this stranger could pop up at anytime and anywhere again because, after all, the twenty-four hours had been long over and this wasn't the movies. This was real. Somebody had been at her house, threatening her with a knife at her throat, insisting on her giving him some damn list. She had no idea about any list. Whenever she hadn't been distracted by Mat, she had thought it through from every possible angle, but always came up with a blank.

The touch of Mel's hand on her arm brought her back to the present.

"I'll be careful," she promised, knowing that she would because she didn't want to be in a scary situation like this ever again.

She gave her sister-in-law a kiss goodbye on the cheek and headed for the door.

"Keep us in the loop," Mel insisted.

She replied a quiet, "Will do."

The walk from Liam's house to the bus stop was only around the block, possibly five minutes, and even though it wasn't a busy street, there was always some traffic. And in her opinion, nobody in their right mind would attack her on a bus or at the bus stop.

Or so she hoped.

She quickened her step as soon as she turned the corner and saw a bus approaching. But before she hopped onto the bus a minute later, she watched a black car driving down the street.

Slowly.

Too slow.

A shiver ran down her spine, and she looked up to the bus driver who stared at her in return, waiting for her to make up her mind. Once inside, she swiped her card and found a seat near the driver, watching the car. It slowly caught up with the bus and was right next to her at the next intersection. She was able to look inside and saw an old couple with a street map.

Relief rushed through her as well as anger. She was annoyed with herself and the situation that she was now seeing things that weren't there. She'd be a nervous wreck by the end of the week.

Tiffany exhaled a long breath and as she looked out the window, her mind went back to her problem at hand. It'd been all about a damn list. The police assumed it was a list of people involved in the drug trafficking or production, but she didn't know where Hudson could've hidden it. Another one of the many curses left her lips as the thought came to mind it'd been Hudson's way of getting back at her because, after all, she'd been the one responsible to get him behind bars for a few months. Again, she wracked her brain about where it could be at her place. The other day, her and Mat had turned her house upside down trying to locate anything. They'd even considered the notion the list wasn't on a piece of paper but something like a tape, a USB, or a disc. But they couldn't even find anything similar to that.

Fifteen minutes later, she hopped off the bus and moved over to the timetable to check for her connection before she sat on a small bench to wait.

Her gaze drifted into the distance where she saw a small travel agency. She smiled as she checked the time. A quick calculation in her head told her that Mat would be close to landing in Queenstown. The police had to give her what she would consider a free pass to leave the country. Ultimately, and although her knowledge of the criminal law was limited, she was the victim of a crime and not the suspect. And she didn't believe the victim had to stay around.

****

Mat's flight back to New Zealand was uneventful. As usual, there'd been some turbulence as they'd approached the southern part of the country. As a helicopter pilot, he'd had to learn about the meteorological reasoning behind it all, about the westerly winds a few thousand feet up, and the northerly at the surface, but his stomach always turned upside down knowing he wasn't in control of the aircraft.

With the time difference, it was late afternoon by the time he arrived at Queenstown, and following a quick check-out, he took a taxi to his new place he'd bought in town a few weeks earlier. Once they arrived, he paid and went into the house with a sense of excitement building inside him. He placed his bag on the floor and pulled out his phone from his jeans pocket.

After a quick call to Adam, he gave his parents a call. He ambled into the lounge room and leaned against the window frame as he admired the view across Lake Wakatipu.

"Matiu. How are you? Are you back home?" his mother asked.

He stepped outside onto the terrace, inhaling deeply. He'd missed the fresh air after the a few days in a big metropolitan city like Melbourne.

"I'm in Queenstown for the rest of the week to get a few things organised."

"So you got the contract with the Australian company?"

Mat bit back a chuckle, hearing his mother's excitement about the possible news. "Yes, we have a handshake deal. It's all in the lawyers' hands now."

"Expect any problems?"

Another smile. "Not at all. Anyway, is Dad around?"

"He's out tonight. Some coach meeting at the school."

Hemi Apanui had been one of the great players in New Zealand Rugby history. He'd retired twenty years ago and following his departure from the game, there'd been plenty of offers from all sorts of businesses. But he'd re-located his family to Sydney to escape some of the attention they'd received at home. For a few years, his income had been from occasional television contracts, but when he'd been offered a coaching job at a local school in Auckland, he hadn't been able to resist. A position he still held and loved.

"Could you ask Dad to give me a call, please? I might need some help moving my stuff from Fox to here."

"When will you start the new company?"

"If all goes through, not for another six months, but there's lots of organisation involved." He moved away from the window and headed towards the kitchen to get a packet of chips. "I'll drive up to Fox on Saturday for a week or two to have someone cover my flights while I get this house fixed up and sort out a helipad around here. Not to mention establishing the loan for it."

"It does sound like a lot of work," she said with some concern.

"But it'll be well worth it considering I'll be back in Queenstown."

"I will come as well when your father comes south to help you in the house. Nothing better than a bit of a female touch."

He grinned. "It most certainly is in need of just that."

After he disconnected the call, he opened the pack of chips and went back to the lounge room. His mouth edged up as he stared at the two camping chairs and the foldout table in the middle of the big room. It looked odd and reminded him that he had to buy some furniture sooner rather than later. He sat on the old camping chair, crossed his legs as he leaned back, and thought of Tiffany. His gaze drifted across the lake to the Remarkables, the mountain range along the shore. A sense of contentment spread through him.

You're about the luckiest man in this world.

He fidgeted in the chair as he took a little box out of his pocket. With a flick of his thumb, he opened it and looked at the necklace in front of him. Carefully, he pulled the pikorua out of the small box and ran the necklace through his fingers. He'd come up with the idea when he rushed through the airport and saw the duty free shops. It hadn't taken him long to figure out what to get her. The jade pikorua was a twist symbolising the strength of the bond between two people, and Mat was certain that there was something between Tiffany and him. He'd make sure to mail it the next day.

He reached over to the small camping table for his phone. Her number was already stored on the speed dial…and she answered after one ring.

The relief at hearing her voice gave him an immediate lift.

"Hi, it's me," he said as he pictured her face, framed by her brown hair.

"My little Kiwi man."

Her voice had given him a lift, but the word *my* did him in. He closed his eyes imagining her on her bed, despite knowing she was at her parents' place.

"Did you just call me little?" he asked with a chuckle.

"In the most complimentary way," she explained without hesitation, but with a soft laugh in her voice.

"I cannot say I've ever received a compliment like this before."

"How was your flight?"

"Boring and long as usual." He paused, hesitating whether to ask about any news regarding the recent events. Carefully, he chose his words. "Hearing your voice is a relief, meaning you've either found the list or the guy hasn't found you, thank goodness."

Her sigh didn't go unnoticed, and he kicked himself for bringing it up.

"No," she replied, the cheer in her voice gone. He waited, confused about the *no* which didn't make sense in regard to his statement, and he gave her the time she obviously still needed.

"No sign of this guy. I'm hoping he's given up on the whole thing or has found the damn list somewhere else." There was another small pause, and he thought he heard a background noise of the soft whistle of a kettle and of a mug being set down. "Dad and I went to the police today."

The words *Any news?* lay on the tip of his tongue, but he knew better than to say them out loud. He opened his eyes, admiring the colours in the sky as the sun was about to set.

"I think Dad wanted to meet Sergeant Harris and get all the information first hand. He was good at asking the right question and such. There isn't any progress, though. They've declared Hudson's death as murder and searched his house from top to bottom. I don't know much about the legal stuff and, to be honest, I don't want to, either."

"I take it you're not a suspect."

The sound of the kettle stopped, and he heard what he assumed was a spoon being stirred in a cup.

"No." She paused before she said, "I looked at airfares before."

He raised his brows. "I love the sound of that."

"Should I look for Christchurch or Queenstown?"

"Queenstown." Searching for the right words, he was silent for a few seconds before continuing. "Baby, what would your reaction be if I'd offer to pay for the airfare?"

There was a moment of silence, which wasn't unexpected. The question hadn't come across as subtle as he would've loved to, but he wanted to see her again so much, it was a constant ache inside him. And if he could help her financially, it might happen earlier rather than later.

"I'd ignore you," she whispered.

"I didn't mean to offend you, you know that, right?"

Another small pause. "I'm not offended as long as you're not offended by my refusal. I know you mean well—"

"Baby, I'm being selfish here. I'm hoping if I pay for the airfare you might come a bit sooner."

"Sooner than when?" she asked with a small laugh.

He chuckled. "As soon as possible."

There was an obvious sigh on the other end of the line. Had he pushed her too far?

"How about I cover the airfare, and you offer me a bed at your place and pay for food?"

"Deal," he replied without any hesitation. "Do you prefer caviar, lobster, or rump steak?"

"Oh, my God, Mat, I'm hoping you're pulling my leg. Keep it simple, otherwise I'll leave and enjoy meals on my own."

"Ouch! You wouldn't do that to me, would you?"

"I'm a simple girl with simple needs."

"You're a lot, but not simple. And *that* is meant in the most complimentary way."

When she didn't reply, he worried she'd misunderstood him.

"Tiffany?"

"Still here. Letting the compliment sink in. Haven't been spoilt with words for a long time."

"Well, get your cute little butt over here and prepare yourself for a twenty-four hour feast of compliments."

"I can't wait. Dad told me a bit about New Zealand, but he's never been to the south island."

"Completely different to the south. Happy to take you to the north as well one day."

"How about one step after the other."

The distinct breathing told him she was thinking about her next words. It took him back to know how well he'd come to know her.

"Tiffany?"

"I'm scared, but looking forward to visiting you at the same time. After all, I've known you for only a few days. Does that make me naïve or you very special?"

He exhaled a long breath. "I'd love to say it makes me special, but I'd say that's the easy answer. Please don't be scared. We clicked straight away, and I'd say the fact that Steve and Liam know me well made you trust me a little faster."

The noise of a chair scraping along the floor and the sound of something like a dishwasher door opening told him she'd finished her hot drink.

"I'm having a small break from my studies at the moment so the timing would be perfect. I'll have a look at flights tomorrow and let you know as soon as I find something. It must be late there."

"Never too late to talk to you. And I'm not that tired. I had a little snooze on the plane."

Her little snort surprised him. "Dad told me about the rotten flight he had both ways when he flew to Auckland."

"It's very common. It's because of the southern air mass—"

"Maaat," she nearly screamed. "Don't tell me it's common, otherwise I might have to come via boat."

That got a laugh out of him. "You'll be fine. Watch a good movie."

"The boat idea sounds better and better all of a sudden," she replied with a chuckle.

"I can come and pick you up with Lucy."

Silence. He knew exactly why, too, but let her wait two or three seconds. "Baby, Lucy's my helicopter."

"I knew that." Her voice was filled with exaggerated conviction.

His laugh echoed in the unfurnished room, which reminded him again he'd have to get a few things down from Fox before she arrived. At least get a decent bed.

"I'm sure you know I'd talk to you much longer, but I've got to get ready. Mum's asked me to help her going through the old baby clothes. She's determined to find a few things for Liam junior to wear."

If that thought didn't pull at his heart. He'd never bothered with children. Of course, he had them on flights, and their excitement was always contagious, but when he was able to, he avoided them. Yet, at that moment, the thought of a small child running around the house with some of Tiffany's old clothes grew on him.

Very much so.

"I miss you," he heard himself saying, surprised at his own acknowledgement.

"I miss you, too. And I promise checking airfares will be on my agenda for tomorrow." And with a little chuckle, she added, "No offence to Lucy, but I'm more of an airplane kind of person."

"I won't tell her, ay," he replied with laughter in his voice. "But she'll be offended if you won't let her show you the mountains around Fox Glacier."

"Oh, my."

"I'll hold your hand all the way."

"Will there be the opportunity of watching movies?"

"Baby, once you fly over the mountains, you don't want to watch movies. Trust me."

"I can't wait."

He replied, "Me neither," and reluctantly disconnected the call. A quick look at his watch told him what his stomach had been trying to tell him for the last fifteen minutes — it was time for some food. He stood, grabbed the keys, and made his way into town, his excitement growing at the knowledge that the woman who'd captivated his heart a few days earlier would be with him soon. Hopefully, very soon.

Eight

INDEED, the first thing Tiffany did the next morning was check for flights. A quick surge of excitement raced through her. It had been only three days that she had spent with Mat, but during those three days she'd been her happiest in a long time, if ever. Heat rose to her cheeks, as she became aware of her constant smile and her pounding heart every time she thought of him. Even when she'd been travelling around Australia, which had brought her to the most wonderful places between the east and west coasts, to the rugged terrain of Tasmania, to some beautiful places in the Kimberley, she hadn't experienced this kind of contentment.

And not even when she'd returned to Melbourne had she felt such an acute loss like the way she did since Mat had left. The few days during which she'd listened to Mat talking about New Zealand, about his job as a helicopter pilot, the people he met, or the loss of his good friend who died in a helicopter accident during a bad storm, she'd experienced some void inside her. Something was missing in her life despite having seen so much already compared to others, and despite having met so many people from all over the world, some of whom she was still in contact with, she'd never been so drawn to a person as she was to Mat. She was sure it wasn't irrational thinking.

There'd been something between them. Something different and so familiar at the same time. The reason for him being in her thoughts constantly, even in her dreams. The thumping of her heart when she heard his voice. Or, the heat rising to her cheeks when she thought of him.

Yet, worry seeped through her as she thought of Hudson. She'd liked him from the start, too, and would've never guessed he had been involved with drugs.

She rolled her eyes at the ridiculous comparison. Mat wasn't anything like Hudson.

She made herself a cup of tea and placed the laptop on the kitchen table before booting it up. But she was easily distracted and searched for places instead. She didn't have to read the description of the photos in front of her, knowing them already from what Mat had told her. A display of beautiful pictures of places like Queenstown, Lake Wanaka, and Fox Glacier made her want to visit the place even more.

Biting her lip as she gazed across the lake, she grew restless on the chair as she thought of exploring those places with him. Mat kissing her again, holding her, and touching her skin. With heated cheeks, she admitted she was looking forward to Mat discovering her body, kissing her in places so few men had kissed before. Then again, so few men had made her feel the way Mat had with one simple kiss.

Focussing back on airfares, she startled a little when a man's hand settled on her shoulder, accompanied by her dad's deep voice, "Don't you worry, darling. We will have you covered with any expenses."

"Dad! I didn't hear you come in." She looked up, heart pounding. "I don't want you to spend so much money on me so you know I'm safe."

He gave a vehement shake of his head. "No, it's not about your safety, because, truth be told, my little girl can't be safer than in my arms or in my house. The reason we'd like to pay this for you is because we know, and we can see it, this is going to make you happy. This is what you want." He scratched the back of his head as he sat next to her. "Even though you think I'm old and I never understood you...I did. And I always will because we are alike." His mouth curled upwards in a smile. "I never liked to follow my dad's advice. I never liked his ideas. I thought I had to do it my way because I was sure my way was the right way."

"Dad—"

He held up his hand. "See, even at my age you live and learn. I know you compare yourself to your brother, but that had nothing to do with it, and everything to do with the wild spirit within you. A spirit that wants to explore and has to see the world. You don't like to be pushed onto a path given by others." He let out a sharp breath. "I hadn't realised I was building that path for you brick by brick. Until recently. Until I saw you coming back from your trip telling me about Australia and all the different people you met. We want to pay this for you because I want to destroy the brick path I laid out for you. I want you to follow your own path."

He leaned forward and placed his hand on hers. "I want to help you position the bricks you choose to walk on."

Tiffany wasn't able to hold back the tears. Never had she heard anything like that from her dad. His choice of words surprised her.

Wild spirit.

Was it as easy to explain as she'd always thought she was competing with Liam when it was simply not in her nature to be like him?

"Dad—"

"Please, Tiffany. At least think about it."

Her lips pulled up into a smile. "Which part? Your poetic speech about the path I'm supposed to walk on or the airfare?"

He shook his head as he let out a chuckle. "Both, I suppose."

"Dad?"

"Yes, darling."

She met his gaze, hesitated, but finally asked, "While you're in this contemplating mood..." She blew out a breath as she looked down. "I know Mat is a really nice person, yet still, I'm a bit anxious."

With a nod, he gave her hand a little squeeze as he replied, "And nobody will be able to take that away for you. You've burnt your hands and trust won't come easy. Healing takes a long time as you have to learn again to trust yourself, your feelings as well as your judgement."

"I'm scared I won't be able to."

He nodded again. "Being scared is not all that bad, it means you'll be in charge of your faculties," he added with a wink.

A smile tugged at her lips as she stood to give her father a hug. "Do you sometimes have regrets?"

His bark of laughter startled her. "Oh, darling, where do I start? It's part of life." He stood as well and took her into an embrace. "I can't think of many, but I do regret not listening to you."

Her father chuckled. "That's what we call maturity."

She snorted and moved even closer into her dad's embrace.

A sense of safety surrounded her for the first time in a long time, and she didn't want to let go.

****

A couple of days later, and a few days earlier than planned, Mat was back in Fox Glacier with his father. It was a mild evening, and they decided to have a drink outside in front of an open fire. Adam had joined them as well.

"Good to see you, Hemi," Adam said, as he raised his beer towards Mat's father. "How are you?"

Mat watched as a smile spread across his father's face and prepared himself for Hemi's usual speech about life after All Blacks and how much he enjoyed the simple life nowadays.

He smiled. So often had he heard about rich sports stars losing their wealth by bad management or no incentive to work. His father, however, had never taken the money for granted and at the same token had taught his two boys to manage money well.

A little while later, Adam finished his beer. When Mat offered him another one, he shook his head. "No thanks. I still have to drive back."

Mat nodded.

"Tell me about your girl, though."

With a chuckle, Mat leaned forward and placed his bottle next to his chair, resting his elbows on his knees. "Weirdest thing. But I can't get her out of my head. She's coming over later this week."

"Will you bring her here?"

"Got to introduce her to Lucy, haven't I?"

They laughed.

"Serious?" Adam asked.

Mat looked over to his father then leaned back into his chair. He hardly knew Tiffany, but something inside told him it could be something serious.

But how would he know how to define *serious*? He'd never felt like this before, had never yearned for a woman like this.

"No idea. You're thinking way ahead of things. We've barely known each other for a few days." He shook his head with a chuckle. "And you're talking serious."

Adam lifted his right shoulder in a shrug. "Never seen you like this before. All this fuss to get things moved. Not to mention that you let Sam take over flights so you have a few days off."

Mat exhaled a long breath and pinched the top of his nose with his thumb and forefinger when he saw Hemi trying hard to hold back a grin. "Fuck."

His father made a loud noise of disapproval, and Mat apologised straight away.

He snapped to his feet. "I'm tired. How about we'll talk about the contract and flight schedule tomorrow. I'll stop by the office at about ten."

Adam's bark of laughter echoed in the clear air, and despite himself, Mat smiled.

The next few days were spent packing. Hemi kept busy following Mat's instructions, and Mat spent most of his time in the office or flying Lucy.
Trying hard not to count down hours until Tiffany's arrival. But, in spite of the constant rush, she was always on his mind. Even while flying, which was usually the time he was able to clear his mind of everything to revel in the beauty of the scenery in front of him. When Adam had thrown the word *serious* into the mix, he'd laughed, but the more he'd thought about, the more he got used to the idea of having Tiffany around for longer. The occasional thought that she might not be the one for him did

occur to him, but he wasn't able to hold on to it. So one night he gave Steve a quick call.

"Mate, how are things? How's the move getting along?" Steve asked.

"Yeah, things are good here. I've got Dad here packing up like crazy."

Steve chuckled. "Poor bugger. You'd think with the money you've made over the years, you could afford a company to do that."

Mat ignored the last comment. His friend had been on his back for years about how he should be spending more money to make his life easier. Mat saw that as a waste of time. His dad was slaving around, but knew how Mat wanted things packed. They were a team.

"Anyway, the reason I'm calling is Tiffany."

There was another chuckle. "I've heard about the travel plans. My little girl is scared out of her brains."

Mat's brows shot up. "How come?"

"Where do I start?" He laughed. "The flight. The water. The fact that she doesn't know you, as well as the fact that, despite everyone telling her what a great guy you are, she's worried."

Concern rushed through Mat. He told himself it had more to do with Hudson than with him and the mere fact of how much she was still healing from the trauma of what had happened the previous year.

"Mate, I'm doing the right thing here, aren't I?" he asked, though with some reluctance.

"Meaning?"

"Meaning…" Mat searched for the right words, but found none.

"Whether you're investing in something that might not work out?"

"Yes," he replied, relieved how much his friend understood him.

"Tiffany's head over heels for you. Once she'll have spent a week with you and is able to put the past aside, you two will have a great time."

Mat raked his fingers through his hair, thankful for his friend's words. Even though he'd had no doubts about how he felt about Tiffany, or at least only little, Steve's assurance put him at ease. "Thanks, Steve. I appreciate it."

"Nah. No worries. You'll be fine. Look after my girl."

"Will do," he replied, a big smile spreading across his face.

Nine

Tiffany checked the time on her phone and looked up at the board again with the flight schedules. Less than an hour until her departure. The airport was busy again with people coming and going. She turned to her parents, and her lips pulled up into a smile.

"I can't believe I'm doing this," she said.

A smile tugged at her father's lips as well. "You're doing it, darling. You're about to fly to New Zealand, and you'll have a wonderful time."

She nodded half excitedly, half hesitantly as she touched the new necklace around her throat. It had come in the mail the day before with a little note from Mat. She'd been more than surprised when she'd opened the small box. With shaking hands, she'd held his handwritten note that explained all about the green coloured jade pikorua, a word she had to practise how to pronounce.

Strength of the bond between two people.

She'd read it a couple of times, enjoying warm tingles spreading through her body. Obviously, it wasn't her imagination that there'd been something between them. A connection or even an attraction.

She looked up at her father, whose smile told her he'd guessed her thoughts.

"Yes, I will," she finally said in response to his comment to have a good time. "So hard to believe that a week ago I had this horrible guy threatening me, and at the same time, I don't know whether I should, in a very twisted sense of right, be grateful to him. I wouldn't be standing here, I suppose, if it hadn't been for him."

"Life moves in mysterious ways and sometimes bad things have to happen before good things can move in. Yet, often we are so wrapped up in the negative, we don't see the positive."

Tiffany raised a brow with a dubious frown. "Dad, where does all the sudden wisdom come from?"

Her father's gaze drifted over her shoulder and into the distance. "Remember when you drove off to explore Australia, and I had mixed emotions, hoping that you would find who you are?" He huffed a grim laugh. "Meanwhile, I was looking forward to having some time when I wouldn't fight with you. Instead, I worried every day and every night. Every phone call we received, I worried it was bad news from you." He met her eyes. "But you had a wonderful time. Of course you did. I should have known, because you're not only determined, but you always knew how to have a good time. Silly old me, I should have accepted that and enjoyed it with you. Through the photos you sent and the stories you told us."

Her mother placed a hand on her husband's arm. "Tim, as wonderful as this all sounds, she'll miss the plane with all your sentimental—"

He shot his wife a mock glare, although he wasn't able to hide the little twitch of his lips and his eyes full of love. "I've been pragmatic for too long. Give me five minutes with my favourite daughter."

"I'm your only daughter," Tiffany commented with a chuckle.

"That doesn't stop you being my favourite," he replied with a grin. "Anyway, I'm not saying all this because you're back in town and studying, but I can see it in your eyes, in the way you speak, and the way you behave, that you found yourself. And in the last few days I've noticed it even more how happy you are. Your mother and I believe there's a little future for you and Mat." He chuckled. "But we're not matchmakers. If it doesn't work out so be it, but I don't think we've ever seen such a sparkle in your eyes or happiness in your words as we have in the last week. You've met the challenge of Hudson's mess dead on. The challenge of being threatened. The challenge of dealing with the police. The challenge to be humble and moving back to your parents. We're proud of you. You deserve this time with Mat, and you'd better tell him if he doesn't treat you right, I'll come over and pick you up myself. But only after giving him some words from a dad who seems to have come to his senses at last."

"Darling, she'll never make it there in the first place, if you don't stop talking," her mother reminded him.

Blinking back tears, Tiffany checked the time again on her phone. "Dad, you're making me cry, and I've made such an effort with my makeup this morning."

"Darling, you look so much better without makeup. Trust me."

She snorted. "You'd like me after five days of camping with no shower at all."

He lifted his shoulder in a slight shrug. "Sue me."

Letting out a long breath, she turned around to look at the flight schedule again. "I think it's time to go."

Her mother nodded. "Yes, I think so, too."

"I've checked the weather this morning; you should have a smooth flight," her father said.

"Good Lord, Dad, don't say that now. I tried to not even think about it."

Tim leaned in and placed a kiss on her cheek but stopped short and instead took her into his embrace for a massive hug. "I love you, darling, and I'll see you in two weeks."

As much as Tiffany relished her father's squeeze, she struggled to put some distance between them, to be able to breathe again. She drew in her lips, trying hard not to offend her father by wriggling out of his arms.

"And don't forget to send me emails with lots of pictures. We don't want Liam to have created one of these addresses for nothing."

Her mother rolled her eyes. "Not to mention the hour he spent explaining to your dad how to use it."

That made Tiffany laugh. She gave her dad a quick kiss on the cheek before she turned to her mother to give her a big hug. "I love you guys. I really do." She took a deep breath, picked up her bag, and stood straight. "But I've got to go." And without any more words, she walked towards the customs hall.

The next half an hour was more or less a blur. First, she was scanned from top to bottom, then she had her bags checked, and last lured into buying all this wonderful stuff which was apparently so much cheaper than outside any airport. When she made it to the gate, she sat, hardly able to get her heart rate under control. Taking a deep breath to calm her jagged nerves, she swiped her damp palms down the sides of her pants and forced herself to stop licking her dry lips. Her nervousness made her heart skip with anxiety. Of course, it wasn't the first time she was going to be on a plane, but after Hudson, it was the first time she was going to spend time with a man. It'd been over twelve months since she'd been near a man. However, the last couple of days she hadn't been able to think of anything other than being kissed by Mat. Or even touched. And just the simple thought of it had her body on full alert. She cupped her hand over her mouth to avoid a cackle at the thought she'd even packed protection.

Just in case.

No, it wasn't just in case. She wanted him. Her imagination had run wild at how it would be to be touched and kissed all over by Mat. She rolled her eyes at herself for her behaving like a teenager.

Trying to distract herself, she stood and walked over to the huge glass window. Planes from so many different countries were coming and going, big ones to small ones. The simple rhythmic diversion of come and go soothed her nerves, and she startled when the announcement came it was time to board. Her heartbeat picked up a notch again, and she sighed as she picked up her bag. The emotions inside her were on a rollercoaster ride. She needed to relax. Yet, queuing in a long line didn't help, and when she finally sat next to a window fifteen minutes later, she was neither calm nor nervous, but exhausted. She held back a yawn during the security announcement, which was done with the help from the All Blacks, and the best she'd ever seen.

She explored the in flight entertainment. The many choices of music, movies, or TV series weren't of any interest to her, and it wasn't long before her eyes drifted shut, tired as she was from all the excitement over the last week, and she fell into a light slumber.

Tiffany woke to the broadcast that they were about to land in Queenstown. She was surprised she'd slept all the way through. Blinking the sleep from her eyes, she focussed on the scenery outside her small window. Instantly, she was captivated by the mountains around her and the valley of their flight path. In awe, she took everything in, from the green valley, the roads, and the snow-capped mountains.

She fidgeted with the buckle to distract herself from the bumpy descent. A smile touched her mouth as her thoughts took her back to Mat. The fact she was going to see him again in only a very short time did that to her. And for a moment, apprehension struck her that he might not be waiting for her. She rolled her eyes at herself for being silly. Of course he'd be there. He'd rung only the night before, telling her about the things he'd bought for the house to make it liveable. There'd been a trace of nervousness in his voice as he told her about his week. He'd even apologised that his parents were still in town for another day. They'd helped him to get organised for her visit, considering the house wasn't yet fully furnished, with most of his belongings still in Fox Glacier. Guilt spread through her that he'd gone through all the trouble just for her.

She recalled his words. "I would've bought a house if that meant I could have you here for a little while."

It had been one of the nicest things anyone had ever said to her. Heat crept into her cheeks at the simple thought of him. If her recent life were a movie, she'd burst into laughter at the ridiculous notion of it all.

And, yet, it was her life and hope for some happiness spread like ripples inside her. The more she talked to Mat, the more strength she found to reconcile with the past to give way for the courage to trust again.

It even appeared that she was off the attacker's radar. She hadn't heard or seen him all week, even when she had been to the house to pack her bag and grab her passport.

Tiffany was healing, and she loved the feeling.

****

Mat parked the car and rushed into the airport. Out of all days, there'd been roadworks today. He checked the arrival board and headed to the international part of the airport. The first travellers were already coming out from customs. When he searched for Tiffany another string of curses left his lips upon realising he'd left the flowers in the car.

"Damn it."

He moved out of the way to avoid bumping into a group of tourists with trolleys everywhere.

A quick glance around told him there wasn't a flower shop in the area. He ran his hand through his hair, down the back of his neck.

"Fancy meeting you here."

Surprised, he shot around, and his mouth curled into a slow smile. Without saying a word, he snagged her around the waist and pulled her closer as he lost himself in her blue eyes. He leaned in, gently touching her lips with his. It took all his strength to pull back and rest his forehead on hers.

"Welcome to New Zealand."

"It still seems a bit surreal."

He laughed and not able to hold back, he kissed her again.

When he finally broke the kiss, he took her hand and placed the other one on the trolley. They walked through the airport to his car, and as soon as Mat opened the car door, he remembered the flowers. He grabbed them off the seat, walked around the car, and stopped in front of her.

"I forgot. Sorry."

"Gerberas, how lovely." She took the flowers. "Don't think I've ever been given flowers before."

He frowned. "Never?"

She shrugged. "Nope. Never."

Stepping closer, he kissed her cheek, knowing if he touched her lips, he wouldn't be able to stop. "I'd better remember that."

Ten minutes later, they drove along the road into Queenstown.

"It's beautiful," she kept saying. "So beautiful. And so different."

Pointing to the snow-capped mountains, he explained, "These are the Remarkables."

"The mountains?"

He nodded. "And this over there is Lake Wakatipu."

"I will have to learn how to pronounce all these places so I won't make a fool of myself."

"Yeh, Lake Wakatipu. Apparently, Wakatipu is a shortened form of Wakatipuwaimaori. Not sure about the meaning, though. Mum would know."

"Well, I'm glad they shortened it," she told him with amusement.

Mat was quiet while he made his way through the busy streets of Queenstown.

"It's a beautiful place, very busy, though," she said when the traffic lessened.

"Yeh, very busy. Lots of tourists here."

When he stopped in front of the house fifteen minutes later, he watched her as she got out and took everything in. He knew it was the odd one out in the area, but he wanted the view and hoped she'd love it as well. He saw his mother and before he was able to get out of the car, she was already coming towards them.

"Kia Ora, Tiffany."

Her gaze met his through the open door, and he grinned as her eyes conveyed her surprise. "I told you my parents are still here, didn't I?"

She nodded. "I didn't expect a welcoming committee. And your mum is...she's..."

"English."

"That makes sense."

Shaking his head, he let out a laugh.

Tiffany arched her back to stretch her spine as she walked towards his mother. "Nice meeting you, Mrs..."

Mat casually stepped out of the car, slammed the door shut, and joined the two women. "It's Apanui," he explained to Tiffany as he placed a kiss on his mother's cheek.

Tiffany blew out an embarrassed little sigh. "Nice meeting you, Mrs. Apanui."

"Call me Harriet." She took Tiffany's hand. "Come on in. Hemi and I won't be much of a bother, and we'll be going back to Auckland tomorrow. Excuse my excitement at meeting you."

"Mum," Mat said softly. "Give her some space. She's probably tired."

"Would you like a cup of tea, Tiffany?"

She nodded. "I'd love one."

"Wonderful. Matiu will show you the house while I start the kettle."

Shaking his head, he smiled as he placed his hand around Tiffany's waist and gently pushed her towards the house. "It needs a bit of work. Let me show you my favourite place in the house first."

Mat noticed her flushed cheeks, and his mouth curved, but he didn't explain.

They entered the house and stepped into the open plan kitchen area to the left.

Tiffany gasped. "Oh my."

He took her hand and led her past the kitchen to the back of the house.

"This room is currently occupied by my parents. So we won't go in there." He stood for a moment before he turned around. "Where's Dad?" he shouted towards the kitchen.

"He's getting a few things for me for dinner."

With a slow nod, he turned back to Tiffany. "Rooms two and three are over there, but empty." With a few long strides, he was at the end of the hall. "My bedroom and this one," he said as he pointed to the last room, "is for you." He took her hand and pulled her closer. "I...I..." He let out a big sigh. "I don't want to push you into something you might not be ready for."

One of her brows arched. "Not ready?"

He chuckled, took her hand, and moved into his room. With a kick, he shut the door behind them before his mouth was on hers. Gentle at first, but when she lifted her arms and wrapped them around his neck, her body pressed into his and their kiss deepened.

"Baby, I've missed you," he whispered against her lips, soaking in the scent of her perfume. She put some distance between them and met his gaze. "I missed you, too." And with a shy smile added, "And somehow I think I'm *ready*."

Warmth rushed through him, something so intense when he realised what she'd said, it unearthed something deep inside him. Something more than desire and lust.

But before he had a chance to respond, he heard his father's deep voice on the other side of the door.

He leaned his forehead against hers. "Bad timing on his behalf," he whispered.

Hesitantly, he let go of her and opened the door.

"I didn't interrupt anything, did I?" Mat's dad said with a big grin as he stepped towards Tiffany. "Nice meeting you. I'm Hemi Apanui."

"Nice meeting you, too," she responded softly.

"I don't usually barge in like this, but I do like giving my son a bit of a hard time," he explained, as he placed his hand on his son's shoulder. "I'd better leave you two be. Just don't get anything started. Your cup of tea is waiting for you in the lounge room."

Tiffany blushed, and Mat rolled his eyes.

"Parents," Tiffany said once Hemi had left the room.

He nodded. "Who would've thought that at the age of thirty I'd still have my parents around when bringing home a beautiful girl?"

She snorted and took his hand. "Let's have this cup of tea."

But before they did, he pulled her closer again to steal another kiss.

They joined his parents in the big lounge room, where she had her cup of tea and endured the many questions from Harriet and Hemi. An hour later, though, she excused herself to take a shower.

"I'm sorry, but I feel sticky from the flight."

"We understand," Harriet replied. "You go and refresh while I prepare dinner."

A few minutes later, there was only a door between him and Tiffany — naked. Mat groaned and rubbed his hands over his face when he stood, but froze when the door opened.

"Oh," was all she said when she saw him in front of her. Covered with only a towel, her cheeks flushed, she muttered, "I forgot the soap."

He groaned as his gaze slid over her body. "You're killing me here, Tiff."

A shy grin spread across her face, and he moved toe to toe with her, cupped her face, and kissed her. Deep and hard as he backed her into the bathroom and perched her on the counter, pressing himself between her legs. He trailed little kisses down her throat, when suddenly he noticed she wasn't touching him.

He looked up and met her gaze. "I'm sorry," he whispered.

She placed a finger on his lips. "Don't be. I like it, but I feel...How about we continue in there?" she suggested with a nod towards the shower.

Heat shot straight to his groin, and he unwrapped the towel, touching her reverently, feeling as though he'd been waiting his whole life for this moment.

Never had he wanted someone as much as he wanted Tiffany, and for the next half an hour they explored each other's bodies as the water cascaded over them.

Ten

THE next morning, Tiffany sat on the terrace and sipped at her tea as she took in the view in front of her. The lake was completely still, with the reflection of the mountains crystal clear in solid colours of blue and white, green and stone like she'd never seen before. It was the most stunning panorama she'd ever seen. Contentment settled in her chest, so intense it almost made her choke. The connection to the land surprised her, yet she didn't push it away, but embraced it. Of course, it'd been less than twenty-four hours, but the few things she'd seen so far made her love the country, made her understand the passion in Mat's voice whenever he talked about New Zealand.

She cradled the cup of tea in her palms as she took another sip.

Everything here was so much more than she'd expected. The massive house, the large balcony, huge kitchen with a big TV to look at, all those rooms, each with a massive window front, big bathrooms, and showers. Oh yes, the showers were spacious, too, as she'd found out. Guilt crept up in her, mixed with some embarrassment as she remembered how she'd fallen asleep on Mat when they'd gone to bed after dinner.

"It's a beautiful view, isn't it?"

Startled, she looked up at Harriet, a smile curving her lips. Mat's mother was probably in her early fifties, but she kept in good shape, and the blue dress she wore showed off her nice figure perfectly. Her wavy hair was held back with a blue headband matching her eye colour. She was a beautiful woman.

"I can't get enough of it," Tiffany admitted.

"The boys still out running?"

Tiffany nodded.

"May I join you?"

"Please, do."

Harriet pulled a chair and sat, but didn't say anything. Instead, she gazed into the distance. They sat in silence for a long while before Mat's mother broke the quiet.

"I'm truly sorry you had to meet *the parents* on your first visit."

Tiffany looked down at her cup, unsure of how much Mat might have told them about the circumstances of how they'd met, she decided not to mention it. They'd had such a nice evening with a flowing conversation throughout dinner the previous night, but it'd been all about everything else, avoiding private questions. She'd learnt about Hemi's rugby career and was teased about her lack of knowledge. Harriet had told the story of how she'd met him during her holidays with her family. She'd been just sixteen. It'd been romantic, scary, and turbulent all at the same time with both trying to keep their relationship out of the media. It'd been different during those days, but the newspapers were relentless even then, especially considering Harriet's age.

Tiffany had loved listening to them. Their bond, between Hemi and Harriet and as a family, was evident. Even though Mat's older brother, Natana, hadn't been there.

Harriet's subtle cough brought her back to the now.

"I thoroughly enjoyed meeting you. I had a lovely time last night," Tiffany replied.

"I am very pleased to hear that. Matiu's very fond of you. I would've been very upset to know we'd be the cause of some—" She paused, studying Tiffany's face.

"I have a feeling if I was bothered by your presence, Mat wouldn't be that fond of me anymore. It's obvious how important you are to him."

She nodded several times. "Yes, I believe you're right." Her gaze drifted back across the lake which glimmered under the rays of the morning sun. "It's so beautiful here. Of course, we'd like to have him closer to Auckland, but when he sent me a video of the house and the view, I told Hemi that Matiu was going to buy the house no matter what."

No words could express how much she agreed with Harriet, so Tiffany stayed quiet.

"Anyway, I'd better pack up. I know the house is still missing most of the comforts, but don't be shy, let Matiu know if you need something. Men can be rather oblivious to women's needs. First thing he bought was this massive TV instead of a fridge or pots and pans. Not to mention a washing machine."

"Oh my, I hope he didn't buy that just because of my visit."

"You'll be right, love. He would've needed these things sooner or later anyway. Now he doesn't have to pack up everything from Fox Glacier, but only the few items he doesn't want to sell."

Tiffany still felt guilty about all the money he'd spent for her. Although it did make sense to sell everything at the west coast, they were still expenses he probably didn't need.

"You have to keep a watchful eye on what he packs when you go to his house in Fox Glacier."

She arched a brow.

"He'll take you there early next week, he told us. Wants to introduce you to Lucy." Harriet paused, her eyebrows shot up. "You know Lucy's his helicopter, don't you?"

Amused, Tiffany replied, "Yes, he's told me about Lucy."

"Thank goodness, otherwise I could've easily started a rumour."

"Sorry, I just wasn't aware we're travelling to the west coast."

"You have to. You have to see a bit more of this beautiful country than Queenstown. There's Lake Wanaka, the glaciers, and I believe he wants to take you to Dunedin as well."

Tiffany took another sip of her hot drink, overwhelmed by the information. Lake something-something, glaciers, and Dunedin. It sounded like a full program. But spending the whole time with Mat was the icing on the cake.

"I look forward to it," she said just above a whisper. "Although I'm hoping that my meeting with Lucy will be strictly down to earth, so to speak."

Harriet laughed, and something inside Tiffany stirred. It was the same laugh as Mat's: a laugh that warmed her heart because it was so genuine and soft.

"You have to let Matiu take you up on one of the glaciers. It's the most wonderful experience. Matiu is a very experienced helicopter pilot. You'll be safe in his hands. And if he doesn't fly Lucy, Sam will. Matiu will let nobody else fly the helicopter."

She bit the inside of her cheeks, worried about the flight. But his mother's words were reassuring. "So, you've flown with Mat?"

"Oh, yes," Harriet replied with a beaming smile. "Lots of times. The first time was dreadful. It'd taken Hemi, Matiu, and Natana over half an hour to get me into the small metal thing, but once we flew across the valley and over the glacier..." She exhaled a long breath and that simple gesture told more than any words.

Tiffany wanted to ask so much more to put her mind at ease, but the deep voice from inside the house announced Hemi. She looked at him when he stepped outside to join them.

"Morena[6], Harry." Hemi leaned closer and placed a kiss on his wife's cheek.

Tiffany stared at him, still surprised by the similarities between father and son, yet most of

---

[6] Good morning.

Mat's character traits seemed to be from his mother. Despite being in his late-fifties, Hemi looked fit and in very good shape, having run ten kilometres with his son without showing any signs of fatigue. The Maori gene was more defined, with his skin a touch darker than Mat's. He wore a similar ta moko over his arm and shoulder. His hair was a bit longer than his son's, and the lines around his eyes were more defined, and like his wife, he always had a smile on his face.

"Good morning, Tiffany. I hope you slept well?"

"I did, thank you."

"Mat's on the phone but promised he won't be long." He pulled a chair closer to his wife and sat.

"Don't get comfortable, Hemi. You need to have a shower and help Matiu with the desk before we leave."

He winked at Tiffany. "Even though she's third generation English, she still hasn't got the kiwi laid back nature in her."

Tiffany watched the two teasing each other with some envy. She thought back to her parents and admitted to herself that, although not as open as the couple in front of her, they had always been treating each other with loving gestures. Warmth spread through her as she imagined herself with Mat like that in twenty years.

The thought jumped at her, surprised her, but at the same time settled her. All the worry she'd had the previous days about coming to New Zealand on her own to meet a man she hardly knew, faded away more and more.

Mat joined them a few minutes later, placing a kiss on her cheek.

"I've found your favourite place," she told him with a smile.

He turned, hands on hips, and stared into the distance. "I had to have the house as soon as I saw this."

"I can see why."

With the same ease as his father, he pulled a chair closer and sat then whispered in her ear. "My second favourite. You showed me my new favourite spot last night."

Heat shot into her cheeks, which apparently he noticed, considering his low chuckle.

He leaned back, crossed his feet at the ankles, and folded his arms. "When's your flight?"

"Two o'clock. I've told your dad to have a shower and help you with the desk."

"Nah, he'll be all right. Enjoy the morning. We can do the desk next time." He looked at Tiffany. "Have you had breakfast?"

She nodded.

"Much?"

Surprised and unsure by the question, she shrugged.

"Good. We will drop off Mum and Dad and go up the gondola to have lunch at the restaurant at the top."

"Wonderful idea," Harriet piped up. "And you have to have a go at the luge."

"Luge?" Tiffany asked.

"It's like a toboggan, but this one's not on ice," Hemi explained as he stood. "You'll love it."

New Zealand, the country of adventure — Tiffany wasn't more aware of it as at that moment. Anxious and excited at the same time about the next two weeks.

****

Mat wasn't able to take his eyes off Tiffany as they rode up the mountain in the gondola. A little quiver at the corners of her mouth told him how tense she was, despite her eyes darting around, indicating the intensity with which she took in the scenery. Suddenly, she startled, and he followed her gaze to the helicopter taking off from just above them to the side.

"Are you going to fly a helicopter from here?" She leaned around a little farther. "Oh, my God, look at this tiny little take-off spot. How can they land and take off on such a small place?"

The side of his mouth arched as he took her hand. "Trent's flying this helicopter. He is one of the most talented pilots around. And, no, this is not where I'm going to have my helipad. Mine will be a little bit farther out of town."

"You know this guy?"

"Yeh, I know this guy. I kind of know most of the people in the tourism business. You need the connections if you want to be successful."

Tiffany met his gaze. "Once you have your business up and running, where are you going to take the tourists?"

He lifted his hand and pointed to the scenery in front of them. "As far as your eyes can see, this is where I take people. Across the lake. Across the Remarkables, and even farther, if they want. There's nothing better than seeing all this from up above." Placing his arm around her shoulders, he said, "I'll take you one day so you can be my consultant for where to go."

"Who says I'm coming back?" she said with a soft laugh.

He chuckled. "Who says I'm letting you go?"

Seeing her now familiar flushing cheeks, he experienced an intense rush of attraction. He wanted to pull her into his arms and not let go. Wanted her body wrapped around him, to taste her soft skin, and feel it under his fingers. He'd been aware of the attraction before, but this time the idea stayed in his mind. It wasn't a flirt or a woman he was drawn to. It was more.

He leaned in to give her a kiss. With his arm around her shoulders, he gently tugged her closer, happy to have her with him. Never had a gondola ride been more exciting or sexier than today with Tiffany.

Once they arrived at the top, they headed straight to the restaurant. Again, he watched with a bit of amusement how she neglected her meal because she needed to take everything in. Watching the people around her, the bike riders racing down the hill, the helicopter coming and going, and the queue of the luge ride.

"That's next on our list to do," he said, following her gaze.

"I can't do that. I know I'm no good."

"Baby, it's not about being good at it. It's about having fun, and trust me, if the little kiddos can do it, so can you." He studied her face. "I'll be right there beside you."

They finished their meals and had a cup of tea before joining the queue for the luge outside. After picking up their helmets, they went on a chairlift that took them a little bit farther up the hill. Eventually, after about ten minutes, they made it onto the track. Mat watched her as she hung onto every word the instructor told her, concentrating as if she were about to ride a Formula One car.

"Baby, relax," he shouted from behind her. "Check out the boy over there. I'm sure he's no older than seven or eight. And he can do it."

She moved the steering bar forward, careful not to take up too much speed. The white knuckles told him how hard she was holding on.

"Would you like me to be in front of you? I'll be with you all the way."

"Oh-my-God," she screamed as the luge sped down the little slope. "Oh...my...God," she shouted again, as she turned around the first curve with increased speed.

A bark of laughter escaped him as he listened to her squeals of excitement. He was sure it was excitement, because their slow drive down turned into a race, with Tiffany taking on the challenge in overtaking all the small children in front of her.

Her screaming didn't stop until they reached the end of the track. After they returned the luge, he took her in his arms, kissed her with so much passion, with everything he had; telling her how much he'd enjoyed the ride.

"Baby, you're about the sexiest thing when you're having fun," he whispered into her ear.

Her arms flung around his neck. "Oh, my God, Mat, I had no idea how much fun this is. Please, I need to do it again." Her delight was obvious, and it was like an aphrodisiac to him. He couldn't get enough. He doubted he ever would.

He gave her another kiss and said against her lips, "Your wish is my command, ma'am."

And for the second time that day, they queued for the chairlift and once more went up the hill for the luge before racing down the track again with him behind Tiffany who screamed like a little girl having the time of her life.

Exhausted but cheerful, they spent a little more of the afternoon in the restaurant for a drink before they returned down the mountain and back to the house later that day. Mat whipped up some dinner. She'd hardly finished her meal when he took her hand and led her to his bedroom.

"Come on. Let me show you my new favourite place in the house."

"Your bedroom?" she asked, looking around.

Stepping closer, he placed his hand around her waist, slow enough to give her time and space to tell him to stop. He stared at her face for a moment, before he lowered his head and brushed his lips over hers, pulling her tighter. His hand moved under her shirt, touching her bare skin.

"Baby," he whispered into her ear. "Yesterday was sex. Today, we're going to make love."

A little whimper escaped her, and he loved the sound. He traced her cheekbone with his thumb and moved to unbutton her shirt. Reeling in the spell hovering over them, he slowly ran his fingers along the back of her bra until he found the hook and unsnapped it to expose her breasts.

"So beautiful," he whispered, as he cupped each of them with his hands.

She touched his lips with hers before placing her hands on his chest. Their warmth was all he needed for his groin to tighten. Slowly, his hands made their way down her body, then he scooped her up against him and carried her to his bed.

When she pulled at his shirt, he didn't resist, letting her draw it over his head. "I want to touch you," she whispered, as her hand followed the traces of his tattoo, down his chest until she found his nipples. He jerked as her intimate touch sent a surge of desire and warmth through him. Easing her down into the pillow, he lay over her. With soft movements, he started to caress, nibbled her earlobe, moving his hands along her arms, over her shoulders, and down to her breasts.

"So responsive," he murmured, moving his tongue over her nipples.

"Mat." Her groan, so sexy and sweet.

He travelled farther down her body, showering her with kisses, trying hard not to miss a spot as he explored her pleasure points.

"Shh," he said as he shifted his weight and placed kisses on her thigh, first one and then the other, before moving up. Tiffany arched towards him, moaning softly as his tongue explored her most sensitive spot. With one slow, knowing stroke he drove her right to the edge, and when he slid a finger into her body, it didn't take much for her to cry out for release.

While she was still trembling, he moved up her body and lowered himself again, gently sliding into her.

Her hands gripped his shoulders. "Mat. I…"

"I want to see your eyes when you come, baby. Please open your eyes for me."

Looking into those blue eyes of hers brought him close to the point of no return. He withdrew, slowly, and entered again. A little faster, and as his pace increased, gentle and teasing, she met him with each thrust. Their bodies were in harmony when he exploded in a downpour of sensations, throbbing through him like ecstasy until they both came.

Long moments passed as Mat held her close against him until her shudders calmed and subsided.

Never had he felt as close to anyone as he had with Tiffany at that moment. The first time he'd met her less than a few weeks earlier, he'd sensed there was something between them that defied description, yet had held him hostage since.

Gently, he tugged her closer and placed a kiss on her forehead. "Definitely my favourite spot in the house now, hands down."

Eleven

A COUPLE of days and heaps of lovemaking later, Tiffany and Mat packed their bags in the car and headed towards Fox Glacier at the west coast. The drive took them up a steep road, which zigzagged to the summit just outside Queenstown. Once they were close to a viewing area, Tiffany had to ask Mat for a small break to take some deep breaths of fresh air. A little queasy, she climbed from the vehicle and stretched.

"You all right?"

She nodded. "Sorry. Yes, just give me a minute or two. My stomach is not used to alpine driving."

Mat chuckled as he gave her a small bottle of water. "Have a sip of water."

Grateful, she took it. "Is the rest going to be like this?"

Another chuckle. "Nah. It'll be smooth sailing from here on."

"Good."

They got back into the car and made their way to the town of Wanaka along Lake Wanaka. Mat parked the car, and they strolled along the main road.

"How about I meet you back here in half an hour while you do a little sightseeing and I organise lunch, ay?" he suggested.

"Perfect idea," she replied and lifted her head to give him a kiss.

Mat walked up a side street, and Tiffany noticed other women staring at him. Jealousy overcame her, mixed with contentment that she had shared the bed with him for the last few days. The simple thought sent a shiver down her spine. She was having the best time of her life being spoilt by Mat. And, not only in bed. He'd made her breakfast, showed her the local sights, cooked her dinner, and on top of it all, made sure she wasn't neglecting her studies.

Mat was the man of her dreams. And she was falling for him. Despite telling herself repeatedly that even though Queenstown might be closer to Melbourne than Cairns, it was still another country.

Tiffany straightened her shoulders and started walking. There wasn't much time to explore the small alpine town, but enough to get a taste of how much she'd liked it. Wanaka was smaller than

Queenstown and equally less busy. A beautiful township nonetheless with plenty of cafés and restaurants looking across the crystal clear lake, as well as a wide open lake front ideal for picnics.

An hour later, they sat by the lake, full after a big serving of fish and chips. Mat wrapped his arms around her from behind as they enjoyed the scenery in front of them. His warm breath teased her neck, and a shiver ran through her.

She leaned into him and said, "I've travelled around Australia and seen the most beautiful places on earth. I'm proud to be Australian and proud to be living in Australia, but I don't think I've ever felt so at peace as in the places you've taken me over the last few days."

"Yeh," he said. "New Zealand is one beautiful country. It's very special as well."

She looked over her shoulder and met his gaze. "No wonder you and your family never settled in Sydney. Don't get me wrong, I like Sydney, but from the little bit I've come to know about you and your parents, I don't believe it was the place for you all to live. Is Auckland as big as Sydney?"

He laughed. "Nah, not even close, but it's a capital with the atmosphere along with it. Mum and Dad live north of Auckland. It's just easier to say

Auckland because nobody really knows the small towns around there, unless you're a Kiwi."

Her gaze drifted back to the lake as she nodded.

Placing a kiss on her temple, he said, "Time to keep going, baby. We still have a little drive ahead of us."

Their drive took them along the shore of Lake Wanaka and over the Haast Pass through some spectacular scenery — rainforest, waterfalls, mountains, and rivers with crystal clear water as well. Tiffany's phone was clicking away as she took photos at every corner. Finally, late in the afternoon, Mat turned into a long driveway towards a house. As soon as she saw the building, she remembered Steve telling her that Mat had renovated an old barn and turned it into a house. She looked around, and it seemed they were in the middle of nowhere, with the snow-capped mountains to one side and the ocean on the other.

"Welcome to my place," he said, the pride in his voice evident. "This is where I live. And this," he explained as he pointed to a big shed, "is where Lucy lives. I believe she's still working hard, but she should be home a little later." He looked up to the sky and added, "The weather is too good of an opportunity to stop flying."

"I take it the weather is important when it comes to flying Lucy?" she asked, but regretting the stupid question as soon as she had said it. "Never mind. Of course it is. Have you ever flown in bad conditions?"

He nodded then frowned. "Yes, I have, and it's scary. It's the most important thing to remember to trust your abilities and to not lose your cool. The weather up there can change in an instant, and it's hard to explain that to people who have no idea about it. They're up there for a good amount of time. Sometimes we take hunters to a little hut, but have to tell them a day or two later we're going to pick them up again because we're expecting a week of nasty weather." He choked back a chuckle. "Often there's a lot of swearing and cursing, and to be honest, I understand their frustration, but their safety comes first. Most of them get it, but some are so obsessed about it. And it's not only the hunters. Tourists or anybody who has invested a lot of money in getting up there. They don't want Mother Nature to interfere with their plans."

She nodded. "I can see where they're coming from."

"Me too, but —" Mat finished the sentence with a shrug, and she understood dealing with disappointed, sometimes angry, customers was one of the drawbacks of his job. It was the first time he appeared despondent.

Not wanting to dampen the mood after such a beautiful day, she placed a hand on his arm and asked, "How about you give me a tour of the house?"

Nodding, he replied, "Let's do it."

They got out of the car, and he took her hand to lead her to his home. What Tiffany saw next took her breath away.

Mat opened the front door, and she stepped into a large living space with a cathedral ceiling.

"Up there used to be the hay loft. It's now my bedroom," Mat explained, as he closed the door behind them.

She let out a soft laugh. "I see you have your priorities right."

He placed his hand on her lower back and guided her farther into the house. "Over there," he said as he pointed to the right, "is the living room. And this part of the house has the kitchen, a small study, dining area, and another three bedrooms with two bathrooms."

Tiffany walked to the living room area, past the huge rock fireplace, her hands gently brushing the top of the couch as she ambled to the massive front window. She took in the panoramic view of the mountains, covered in snow and lit by the sunlight shining through the clouds.

"And you're really going to move to Queenstown and leave all this behind?"

"Who says I'm leaving it all behind?"

Startled, because she hadn't noticed him behind her, she turned, but instead of meeting his eyes, her gaze drifted towards the vaulted ceiling and the exposed beams. "What do you mean?" she asked, just above a whisper.

He hooked a finger under her chin and moved her head so she had no choice but to make eye contact. "I worked on this house for about three years. I love it. I'm not leaving it."

"I thought you were going to move to Queenstown?"

"I will, but that doesn't mean I will leave all this behind."

She opened her mouth, but no sound came out. The idea that Mat had enough finances to afford both houses had never entered her mind. She was impressed how humble he was despite the money he obviously had. Even though he had a business, she never thought a small helicopter business in a small town like Fox Glacier would be so lucrative. It was a bit intimidating considering she hadn't achieved much in life...yet. She figured his father would've earned a lot of money as an All

Blacks rugby player, but vaguely remembered Mat telling her Hemi had helped him financially with the setup of his business, but not more.

His gentle kiss pulled her back to the present. "A penny for your thoughts."

Shaking her head, aware of her flushed cheeks, she rushed her reply, "Nothing."

"I will still need to come back here once in a while. After all, half of my business is here."

She nodded. Probably too quickly.

"Baby, what is it?"

Tiffany rubbed her left temple. "I'm sorry. The fact that you have lot of money just sank in. I'm not used to it."

"I haven't made you uncomfortable, ay?" he asked, with obvious concern in his voice.

"No. No, not at all. It's…it…" She shrugged. "It's a new experience for me." Placing her hands on his chest, she leaned closer and placed a lingering kiss on his lips. She kissed him slowly, enjoying every second of it as well as his hands, which had moved around her waist, pulling her tight. When she slowly withdrew her lips from his, she whispered, "I'm glad you're not selling this house."

****

The next day, Mat watched Tiffany as she headed to the bathroom. The side of his mouth edged up at the thought he was about to join her in the bath, but a grin followed when he heard her familiar *Oh, my God* scream. With a few long strides, he stood behind her.

"What's wrong?"

Pointing at the freestanding bathtub, she whispered, "A bath with a view."

He wrapped his arms around her and pressed a kiss on the top of her head. "I designed it."

"I love it."

I love you.

Surprised at the last thought, he closed his eyes, and let the three words settle in his head. Gave it room, because he liked it. Very much so.

"Well, get in then. I'll join you in a minute," he heard himself saying, his voice sounding throaty even to him.

They had spent most of the day in Fox Glacier, where he introduced her to Adam and his staff, but also excused himself for two hours to catch up on business. Fortunately, she'd been more than happy to explore the small village on her own. Alas, they hadn't been able to fly Lucy because of bad weather. But he'd made sure he booked a time slot a couple of days later after checking the weather forecast. He couldn't wait to take her up into the air.

After lunch together, they had walked up to the edge of the glacier. No wonder she was looking forward to a long hot bath. Little did she know what he had in mind though, once he joined her.

His phone buzzed in his jeans pocket. He considered ignoring it, but checked the ID and saw it was Steve. Moving out of the bathroom and towards the other end of the house, he pushed the button to answer.

"Steve, how are you?"

"Is Tiff around?"

The way the words were spoken and his friend's tone put Mat on full alert. Something was wrong. And he didn't like it. His gut told him to prepare himself.

"She's having a bath. What's up? Need to talk to her?"

"Are you able to give her some bad news? Or would you rather get her?"

"Pōkokohua [7]."

There was a moment of silence before Steve asked, "Which way, mate?"

"Shoot."

"Tim, Tiff's dad, is in hospital with a heart attack."

---

[7] (an insulting swear word).

Mat froze. Not able to form a word, let alone a sentence, he listened to his friend.

"Happened this morning when he grabbed Tiff's mail."

Steve went on to say that her father had been assaulted when picking up Tiffany's mail earlier in the day. Cold anger crept up inside Mat as well as a sudden, overwhelming rage when he figured out the reason behind it all.

"I had the feeling this was sorted."

Steve's sigh told him half the story. "We all did. There was no sign of anybody the whole time. We took turns getting the mail, thought we were safe. Even the police agreed."

The cursing and swearing that left his lips made even him blush, but he wasn't able to hold back and needed to get it out before telling Tiffany about it.

"Mate," Steve interrupted him. "Do me a favour and clean that filthy mouth first before talking to Tiff."

"I hope this guy rots in hell."

"Get Tiff to call Liam, and they can sort out what she wants to do."

"Will do."

Mat disconnected the call and rubbed his hand over his face as he closed his eyes to clear his head, aware of his curled fists and the throbbing blood in his temples as he suppressed the urge to punch something. He waited until it had passed. He sauntered back to the bathroom, his heart aching at the sight of Tiffany covered by the bubbly foam. He didn't want to be the one telling her, and it broke his heart to destroy the moment.

"Baby," he whispered, "I need you to get dressed. We need to talk."

Twelve

EVERYTHING inside Tiffany clenched when she heard Mat's gruff voice. A rush of unwelcome emotions swayed her, and she was unable to sort them in her head. It was as if her ears had taken in his words, but her brain wasn't able to process them into a meaning. Into something that made sense to her. Despite the water being warm, a cold shiver ran down her spine.

Need you to get dressed. We need to talk.

Surprised, she repeated the words in her head again, but whichever way she looked at it, she was unable to sort them.

And why had he avoided looking at her? She tried to recall what had been said. Or what she had said or done, but nothing obvious came to mind. Had he found something in her diary? But she wasn't able to remember anything she'd written in it that was bad. More the opposite. Had he, by any chance, read the small note that she was falling for him?

She stilled for a moment as she remembered his phone ringing before. Fear and worry shot through her as she thought of her family. She stood so abruptly the water splashed over the side of the bath and all over the floor.

Stepping gingerly out of the tub, Tiffany was in such a hurry she didn't bother to towel herself completely dry. In a rush, she slid her legs into the track pants and grabbed her T-shirt before she went in search of Mat.

Standing against the window with his arms outstretched, his head was bowed.

"What's wrong?" she wanted to know.

He didn't move, which made her even more nervous.

"Please tell me what's wrong. I need to know."

Silence hung like a blanket in the air. Heavy silence.

Instead of replying, he turned, took her hand, and pulled her into his arms. The way he held her in his arms and hugged her, she knew there was something he needed to tell her. Something bad. And she wasn't sure she wanted to know.

His hand moved up and down her back when he placed a kiss on her forehead. "You need to call your brother," he whispered against her skin. "Your dad is in hospital."

Her gaze shot back to meet his gaze, sure his eyes were glistening, telling her he was struggling with something.

"Oh, my God, Mat. Tell me what happened."

"Baby, he's fine, but it's not for me to tell you what's happened. Use the phone in the study and call your brother."

Tiffany looked around, unable to hold back her tears any longer, and ran to the study. Grabbing the phone, she asked him for the Australian country code. But her hands were shaking so much she wasn't able to push the buttons. Mat came by her side, took the phone out of her hand, and paused with his fingers over the numbers.

"What's his number, baby?"

She sobbed out the phone number and watched him as he called her brother. He checked the connection before handing her the phone. Her hands clammy, she had to hold the phone with both hands not to let it slip through her palms. Tears still ran down her cheeks, and she sat as soon as she heard Liam's quiet voice.

"It's Tiffany."

There was a moment of silence during which she heard his breathing. Obviously, he was also struggling with whatever he had to tell her.

"Dad's in hospital, Tiff. He had a heart attack this morning."

She swiped her tears with the back of her hand, trying hard to stay focussed. "No," she murmured.

"Sis, he collected your mail this morning and the bastard wanting the list was there again."

"No. No, please, no." Her tears turned into sobs. Unconsciously, she noticed Mat's hand on her shoulder before he pulled her closer to wrap his arms around her.

"Your neighbour saw the whole thing and rang the police officer…Harris, who must've raced there, because he was at the house within a very short time. Fortunately, because by then Dad was already struggling."

"Dad," she sobbed.

"He's fine, Tiff. Recovering like a trooper. We weren't sure whether to tell you or not, but—"

"No. No, thanks for telling me. I'm coming home as soon as I can."

"There's no need to come home—"

"I need to, Liam. Please understand. I need to be there for Mum and Dad. It's my fault." Again, she wiped the tears, this time with the edge of her shirt.

"Tiff, honestly—"

"No. No discussion."

She heard her brother's long exhale but was sure it was what she wanted...what she needed to do. Mat brushed away a tear with his thumb, and she looked up to meet his gaze. He'd been such a rock the last fifteen minutes she'd almost taken it for granted.

"I'm sorry," she mouthed.

Instead of replying, he placed a gentle kiss on her forehead.

"Tiff? Still there?"

"Yes," she whispered.

"If there can be some good news, I'd say it's that the police found the infamous list. Hudson sent a USB via snail mail, but with the incorrect address so it took longer for it to get to its destination. It's now with the police. I haven't caught up with them yet, but they want to move swiftly to end this whole nightmare for you."

Her brother's words should've caused her some relief, except an emptiness took hold of her. She closed her eyes, absorbing the intensity of it all. And as Mat stroked his fingers through her hair and pressed a soft kiss on the top of her head, the peace she'd experienced in Queenstown as well as Wanaka flowed through her body.

"Thanks, Liam. I'll stay with Mum and Dad anyway until Dad's okay."

"No worries, I understand. Let me know when you get back, and I'll pick you up from the airport."

"Thanks, Liam. How's Mel going? Please tell me she didn't stress too much."

"All going well. She's handling it okay."

"Thank God. So sorry for all of this, Liam," she whispered.

"Not your fault, Sis. By the way, how's New Zealand?"

Her voice grew more upbeat. "It's beautiful, Liam. So beautiful."

"I've never been to the south. Time to put that on my list to do, I'd say."

"Mat's a great guide," she replied, as she met his gaze.

"I'm sure he is. Anyway, I'll see you soon. Love you. Have a safe trip back."

She disconnected the call and rested her head against Mat's chest, closing her eyes as she savoured the scent of him, and again, a sense of security surrounded her. Silence filled the moment, only broken by the sound of the wind whistling around the house.

"Want me to check flights?" he asked, with sadness in his voice.

Not able to look at him, she nodded into his chest and took a deep breath. "I love it here. I love being with you." She paused. The words *I love you* on the tip of her tongue. "But I have to go home to see my dad. I have to, Mat."

"I know," he whispered. "There'll be many more days for us to enjoy together."

She'd been so scared to trust a man again, scared to love, but knowing how much Mat cared and understood made her fall for him even a little bit more.

Made her love him.

Made her believe she'd be able to face the challenges ahead of her.

Thirteen

SAYING goodbye to Mat after their time together was like having someone ripping the floor from underneath her and her falling into a void. The helplessness of it all took her breath, with her heart pounding as she tried to form a simple sentence, but nothing came across her lips. How much she wanted to express the feelings she had towards him, but wasn't able to move.

She wanted to step into his arms and never let go. Ever.

A lot of promises had been made over the last few days, and she hoped most of them would be kept. If not…if not, she'd still have her memories. The memories of a cut-short holiday to this amazing country, and memories of spending some unforgettable days with Mat.

He pulled her closer into his familiar embrace. "Give me a bit of time to get things sorted at this end, and I'll come for a visit."

She nodded, still not able to say a word.

"Baby, you're doing the right thing. I had you for a little while, but now your dad needs you."

Letting out a long breath, she tilted her head to meet his gaze. "There's just too much guilt inside me to cope," she whispered.

"Don't. Don't feel that way. You'll be fine. There's always a calm after the storm."

"And a lot of destruction."

His chuckle vibrated in his chest. "Ko nui taku aroha koe.[8]"

"It sounds so beautiful. I hope you didn't call me a whiny woman."

Mat moved his hands up her arms and across her shoulders before he cupped her face. He brushed her lips with his. "Believe in yourself," he murmured against her skin. "And you'll find that all will fall into place." He took her pikorua necklace between his thumb and finger. "And know I'm always with you."

"Oh, my God, Mat. How am I supposed to keep it together when you talk like this?" Tears ran down her cheeks, but she didn't care.

He leaned in and touched her lips with a tender and searching kiss. She didn't want to let go. She didn't want to leave.

But her parents needed her.

---

[8] I love you so much.

After a long moment, he broke the kiss and whispered against her lips, "It's time, baby. I'll call you tonight."

Without any further words, she took a deep breath, stole another quick kiss, before she headed to the departure lounge via immigration. She tried to distract herself by browsing the few shops, but in the end, it didn't have the desired effect, and she made herself comfortable near the gate and took in the scenery. She reminisced the few days she'd spent with Mat in this beautiful country. Not only had she fallen in love with the man, but with New Zealand as well. A new feeling for her, which scared her and made her float at the same time.

It was time to go back to reality.

Four hours later, she was back home with Liam waiting for her at the airport. He brought her up to speed on her father's health as they drove straight to the hospital. Fortunately, Tiffany was able to visit him for a small while.

She rushed beside him, pulling a chair close, and sat. "I'm so sorry, Dad. I never meant for this to happen."

Her father placed his hand on top of her head, stroking her hair. "It's not your fault, darling, but a sign of the times. Blame Hudson for involving you in this whole predicament."

She wiped a tear away. "I shouldn't have gone to New Zealand."

"Nonsense," he replied with a wave of his hand. "Now wipe those tears, take a deep breath, and tell me all about it. By the way, I am very angry that you came home early," he finished with a wink.

"Dad, you've just had a heart attack."

"So they've told me." He chuckled.

"This is serious."

"They've told me that as well, but none of this has anything to do with your holiday."

With a shake of her head, she started to tell him all about New Zealand — the snow-capped mountains, the deep blue lakes, the many bridges, the green scenery, and that she never got to fly with Lucy, but would do that the next time she was going to visit. And even though her father had his eyes closed, she knew he was listening.

At eight o'clock, the nurse knocked and entered the room, telling Tiffany that visiting hours were over. She nodded, placed a kiss on her father's forehead, and quietly left the room.

Feeling a little bit more at peace, yet aching for Mat.

****

The next few weeks were busy ones for Mat. Due to illness of a few pilots, he had to fill in some of the scheduled flights in Fox. And thanks to a decent weather system over the southern island of New Zealand, they were booked out for most flights. He took on the thirty-minute scenic flight over the Southern Alps, Fox Glaciers, and the crevasses with a landing in the snow above the icefalls. His favourite part was the view of Mt. Cook. It was the best job in the world. The tourists were good fun as well. Even the female ones who flirted their hearts out with him.

But he had Tiffany on his mind, and flying was the best distraction for him. Each night he returned home to his empty bed to his own thoughts and knew there would be neither sleep nor comfort for him. He missed her, ached for her company.

With a cold beer in his hand, he walked through his house and looked around. It was furnished with no expenses spared. Everything spoke of money, yet, why did it leave him so empty? He'd worked hard, had come far even without his father's money, and he had made it on his own. His life was good, and with the start of a new business in Queenstown, it was going to be even better. Women loved him, but he only wanted one. One very special one, living in Melbourne, Australia.

He pulled his phone from his pocket and dialled the familiar number.

"Baby, how are you?" he asked, as soon as she picked up.

"It must be late over there."

The sleepy sound of her voice did things to him. Unsure of what it was, but every cell in his body was drawn to her.

Instinctively, he checked the time. "Busy day."

"Lots of tourists again?"

"Yup. How's your dad?"

He was sure he heard a small sigh before she replied, "He's settled well back home. It's still tough on Mum, but it seems they're both coping very well. Mum's got all the medication under control, and Dad is a picture perfect patient."

"Sounds like he's in good hands."

"Yes, he is. Liam and Mel will look after him on Saturdays, and I'm on care duty on Wednesdays to give Mum a break. So much to take into consideration after a heart attack."

He took a quick sip of his beer as he sat on the couch staring into the darkness outside. "How are you holding up?"

There was a moment of silence, but he didn't push her, knowing she had a big adjustment in her life as well.

"I've moved back into my house. I agreed to it with the police. We're...hoping he's coming back." She stopped and, in just above a whisper, told him, "But I'm so scared. Even with the police on call. I'm sure I'm seeing things where there isn't anything. It's frigging ridiculous. I'm...I'm..."

There was a pause, and he could hear her choking back a sob. His heart ached, and he pinched the bridge of his nose to control the tension building inside him. All he wanted was to get on a plane and fly to be with her. Hold her in his arms and protect her. Where was Liam? Or Steve? Did they really agree to this madness?

"Baby?"

She exhaled a long breath. "Sergeant Harris came by yesterday. There's still no news. This...this guy still walks around, and I wish he had the nerve to come by again so the police can finally catch him. Living in limbo is driving me insane."

There was another pause. He stood and walked over to the window, hoping the still of the night could give him some balance. He was scared, too. Selfishly scared, because he was able to feel her slipping out of his grasp and he couldn't do anything. She needed someone next to her, yet, he was thousands of miles away and in another country. The helplessness and inability to do anything tore at him.

"I have no idea how I got into all this mess," she whispered. "Apparently, Hudson was part of this drug dealing business but wanted out. He must've threatened them to let him live a nice, crime free life or he'd hand a list of all his partners to the police. Idiot that he was took a copy of it and mailed it to me with the incorrect house number." She paused again, and Mat wondered whether it was a coping mechanism. Tiffany was obviously still dealing with the circumstances of it all.

He drew a long breath. "I'm heading to Auckland next week, but could come over for a few days."

"Mat?"

"Yes, baby."

He heard her soft breathing. He hoped he'd calmed her a little, by talking to her, or by simply by listening to his voice. Her breathing had become steadier, and it settled him as well.

"I'd love to be with you again, but..." She sighed. "It's hard to live in this stupid reality and then having you here dreaming of what could be, yet losing focus on what's going on."

He didn't understand. Was she telling him not to come? His head was throbbing and he massaged his temples with his fingertips as he tried to figure out what she was saying.

There was a slight hesitation and what sounded like a tiny tremor in her voice when she spoke again. "Give me a few weeks, Mat. Let them use me as bait, which might be hindered if you were here. I need to sort things out. I need to make sure Dad gets well and catch up on my studies. I need this guy to get arrested so I'm not scared anymore."

He nodded, aware she wasn't able to see him, but there was nothing he could say. Even if there had been, he wasn't sure whether his voice would let him.

"I miss you," she whispered. "I miss you terribly, but I hope you understand I'm busy, I'm tense, I'm tired, and I'd hate for a wrong word to destroy what we have." He heard her soft sobs. "I know you're patient and caring, but I know myself better. Please, don't be mad, Mat."

"I'm not mad," he replied. "More disappointed."

"I need to do this."

It was like a kick in his gut. He had finally found the girl he wanted, and she was slipping through his fingers. Her voice had been fragile when she'd said *"Give me some time."* He was happy to give her time, but scared that over time she'd forget him.

"Okay," he agreed with a hushed voice. "I'll wait. Give me a call when you're ready."

"I promise I will."

He disconnected the call and damn him if he didn't notice a tear on his cheek. This was going to be the longest wait ever. Despite the cooler weather and late night, he opened the door and stepped out onto the terrace. Inhaling deep breaths, he tried to calm down, tried to understand how much she needed the time to get her life back on track.

Desperate for her not to forget him.

Fourteen

WHEN Tiffany slid behind the wheel of her car the following Wednesday, she was about to start the engine when someone grabbed her arm and jerked her out of the vehicle. Screaming, her instinct kicked in and she dived for her phone. But in vain. Her knees buckled under her as she was dragged onto the driveway, hitting the concrete hard with her legs and hips. Waves of pain washed through her when she threw her arms at the person, trying to get away from the situation. Fear shot through her when she recognised the voice. It was the same deep voice from weeks earlier, and she knew she had to fight hard and hope the police would be coming soon — exactly as they had explained.

"We have a car positioned just around the corner," she heard Harris in her ear.

Terrified, she kicked as hard as she was able to, tried to hit her assailant with her fists as often as she could, and hoped to God Harris would come through with his promise. She screamed, but he tightened his grip around her throat, choking the air from her lungs.

"You know what I want. You've had enough time." His eyes gleamed with hatred as they met hers.

And despite her fear, a measure of relief rushed through her and her heart pounded in her chest as she heard the police car screeching to a halt in front of the house.

The next few minutes were like a blur with everything happening like a whirlwind in front of her. One of the police officers pushed her attacker away from her and overcame him quickly, clicking on the handcuffs with ease.

Tiffany tried to catch her breath as she closed her eyes and leaned against the car, flinching when someone placed an arm around her shoulder. Her eyes flew open.

"Shh, it's over now," Constable Jones whispered as she moved her hand up and down Tiffany's arm to calm her. "It's over, Tiffany. We've got him."

Tears of relief ran down her cheeks and, unable to hold back, she simply leaned against the police officer and sobbed, thinking repeatedly, *It's over.*

Jones helped her up on her feet and slowly guided her back into the house. "One of the officers has just rung your brother. He'll be here in a few minutes."

They stepped into the lounge room.

"Where's the kitchen, Tiffany?"

She looked up, confused, before the words sank in, and then she pointed towards the door. "To the right and down the hall."

She sat on the couch, her throat dry like sandpaper and her heart still beating like mad. Taking in a few long, deep breaths, she flinched when the door opened, but eased back into the couch when she saw Harris.

"How are you, Tiffany?"

Tears rolled down her cheeks again. "Like an emotional wreck. Happy and scared at the same time."

He nodded, and a small smile spread across his face when they heard the kettle whistling in the kitchen. "Will you need a medical check-up?"

She declined. "They won't be able to fix what's wrong with me."

He sat on the single seater. "What do you think is wrong with you?" he asked, caring and calm.

Holding up her shaking hands, she replied, "I'm a wreck. Look at me. This guy turned me into a wreck."

Harris took her hand. "It's the adrenaline letdown. Once your brother is here, you should take some pain relievers. It'll help to calm you down."

Jones came in with a cup of tea, and Tiffany was grateful for it. "You should take a pain reliever—"

Harris nodded. "Already advised her of that."

He let go of her hand and stood. "Jones will stay until your brother arrives. I will need a statement, but I think we can leave that until later this week."

Tiffany nodded, took the cup, and sipped the tea when Jones handed her two pills.

Even though she'd known this day would be coming, it'd been scary, exhausting, and a rollercoaster of emotions. Would she ever be able to sleep through the night again? Trust anybody?

She thought of Mat, and wasn't sure what the emotion was that spread inside her.

Closing her eyes, she blocked the noise from outside, leaned back into the couch, and sipped the tea.

****

It took Mat a moment to orientate himself when he noticed his phone was buzzing. A quick look at the alarm told him it was just past two o'clock in the morning. He grabbed the phone and checked the ID.
Steve.
Shit. Worry bolted through him.
"Mate, what happened?" he asked, by way of answering the call.
"Sorry for calling so late, but I've just come home. I contemplated—"
"What happened?"
"You've fallen real hard, haven't you?" Steve replied with a little chuckle. "All good. In a way, anyway. The bastard came back today. The police were able to intervene straight away, and Tiffany more or less only suffered shock."
Mat threw himself back onto the pillow and raked his free hand through his hair. The small distance between Melbourne and Queenstown suddenly seemed larger than from the earth to the moon. He would've given anything to be by Tiffany's side and comfort her. Let her know he was there for her. *Only suffered shock.* The few words stuck in his mind, and he tried hard not to scream out in frustration.
"How is she?" he asked, as calm as possible.

"She's okay. She slept most of the day, had a quick medical check-up because of her injuries on her legs, and has to deal with the shock."

"Fuck. What injuries?"

"She was jerked out of the car, hit the driveway hard, and sustained a few bruises. But she's fine. You should know her. She's a little trooper, thinking positive because she can now go on with her life."

"What about the guy? Is he behind bars?"

"I'd say so. They say they have enough evidence to pin the murder on him, definitely both assaults on Tiff, as well as the one on her father." He paused. "I'd better go. It's been a long day. Will I see you soon?"

The question threw him. Was that a request to come over? Or was he saying something between the lines? Or was Mat simply reading too much into the question? He looked up, trying to find the right words.

"She misses you," Steve said before Mat was able to say anything.

"I miss her, too," he confessed. "And it bugs the shit out of me that she had to go through this on her own."

"Hey, mate, easy. We were here."

Smacking his forehead, he replied, "Sorry, I didn't mean to imply…I talked to her a few days ago and suggested I'd come over, but she said she needed to go through this on her own."

"Yeah, that sounds about right. Her father and Liam gave her a good speech about that yesterday. Trust me when I say, give her a call again."

A smile pulled on Mat's lips. How much he enjoyed hearing those words.

"Thanks, mate. Will do."

Mat disconnected the call and switched on the light. It was the middle of the night, but he knew he wouldn't be able to get much more sleep. There were too many thoughts in his head and too many questions he needed answered. He threw back the duvet and got up.

Ten minutes later, he sat in the kitchen with the laptop and a cup of coffee in front him. He would call Adam in the morning to clarify a few. His friend wouldn't be impressed that he'd be leaving again for a few days, but hopefully he'd understand. Searching through the web, he found a flight later that day via Auckland to Melbourne arriving early the next day…a couple of clicks and the flight was booked.

Mat wasn't sure what to expect, but he knew he wanted, no, *needed* to see Tiffany again. Hold her in his arms and help her through the rough times she was currently dealing with. The picture of someone jerking her out of the car and injuring her played in his head repeatedly, and it made him sick. He opened up a picture of her on his laptop and traced her face with his finger. He missed her so much and hoped she'd like the idea he had come up with during the last few days.

He checked the time — close to five o'clock. Enough time for another snooze before he'd get ready for his travels.

Fifteen

IT took Tiffany a long time to get out of bed. Every bone in her body ached. The memories of the other day were shoved to the very back of her head. That was in the past, and she desperately tried to look forward to the future now. Hudson was gone, the list was gone, the attacker was in prison…it was time to refocus and move on.

And she hoped the future would include a certain person.

After a brief shower, she prepared some breakfast and ate it in bed while watching the news. She was tired. Exhausted. The whole drama had taken a lot out her, but the last few weeks had been very busy for her as well. Twice a week she'd taken her father to rehab and every other week for a swim. The rest of the week, she'd studied hard, got as many assignments done as possible, and was close to finishing her diploma.

There wasn't a day when she didn't think of Mat. Goddamn, she missed him. She missed him with such intensity, her body ached all over. She wished he'd been there with her yesterday, to hold and comfort her. But simply his voice would've done the trick.

She placed her cup on the bedside table and stretched the tiredness out of her bones before switching on her phone.

No messages.

She was about to give Mat a call to tell him how much she missed him and about the attack when she remembered Steve had already called him late last night. She checked the messages again, as well as other private message apps.

Nothing.

Close to tears, she placed the phone back on the bedside table. Mat obviously had more important things to do than check on her. With the weight of the whole world, she threw herself back into the pillow, letting the tears flow, once again regretting the decision to ask him not to come to Melbourne. Again, when everyone said go right, she'd chosen to go left.

A knock at the door startled her back from her thoughts. She checked the time. It was just after ten o'clock. She'd agreed with her parents and brother there would be no visits until she felt well enough. Her mother hadn't liked the idea, but understood that Tiffany needed some space and time to digest what had happened, but also to heal, mentally as well as physically.

Another knock.

Tiffany got out of bed and headed towards the front door, aware that she was dressed in a lousy T-shirt and some panties.

Mat's T-shirt.

She opened the door, but left the chain hooked.

"Mat," she whispered, the surprise of seeing him in front of her leaving her speechless and trembling with anticipation. Her knees went weak, while her heart skipped a beat.

He cocked a brow as he took her in, especially her outfit. "Can I come in?"

The mere sight of him had her body reacting with every nerve cell. Despite knowing how much she'd missed him — so very much — seeing him in front of her door was like the vision she needed. Without thinking twice, she closed the door, unhooked the chain, opened the door wide, rushed towards him, and threw her arms around him, placing a quick kiss on his lips.

"If I had known this was the welcome, I'd have come much earlier."

She let out a choked laugh. "I missed you."

"I missed you, too, baby. So very much." He placed his arms around her waist and tugged a little closer. "How are you feeling today?"

His breath tickled the skin just below her ear, and she remembered how she'd enjoyed being in his arms.

"Much better now that you're here."

"How about we go inside? Unless—"

"No. No *unless.*" Slowly, she moved her hands past his shoulder, down his arms, and took his hand. "C'mon in."

She closed the door behind him and noticed how nervous she was by swiping her clammy palms on her T-shirt.

His T-shirt.

Taking a step closer to him, she studied him. Something was different. Not only was he avoiding her gaze, but his hands were in his pockets. Was he here to tell her that their short-lived romance was over already? Had she made a fool out of herself by jumping at him like a desperate woman? Her stomach tightened and suddenly her excitement turned to anxiety. So she went for broke.

"I was dreaming of you last night."

A smirk pulled upon his lips as he finally met her gaze again. "Tell me about it."

She didn't move. "Actually, I've been dreaming of you every single night."

"It's the magic T-shirt. I've been looking for it."

A snort escaped her. "Yeah. Sorry. I stole it before I left."

With two long strides, he stood in front of her, reaching for the necklace he'd given her. "A necklace. My T-shirt. I'd better watch out or you'll take something else from me."

Tiffany placed her hands on his chest, aware of the heat spreading through her body. "Well, it's nothing compared to what you stole from me."

His brows shot up, his eyes widening the barest fraction. "Me? I wish I had. All I have is a few photos on my phone."

She pinched her lips together, tilted her head to look at him. "You stole my heart," she whispered. But she didn't let him reply. Instead, she brushed her lips over his. "There should be serious consequences for that."

His chuckle against her skin made her body shiver. Even though, she still wasn't sure whether he'd stopped by for a visit, she was sure she wouldn't let him go again.

Her life had gone from second gear into fifth within weeks. Her ex-boyfriend had been murdered. She'd been threatened with a knife. She'd met Mat, flown across the sea to be with him, and almost lost her father. It'd taken weeks for her to work on her guilt which had crushed her from all corners. Counselling had helped a lot, and she wasn't giving up on that, but throwing herself into her studies and being busy assisting her parents had helped as well, because she'd had a goal — watch her father's health improve and finish as much of her studies as she was able to before the end of the year so she could go back to spend more time with Mat.

Instead...instead, he was here with her.

He slid his fingers into her short hair and held her gaze, studying her face, before he leaned in to kiss her. His kiss was so tender and sweet, yet the fire it created was anything but. Her heart raced at his touch, emotions surging.

She let out a shriek when he scooped her up into his arms, and carried her to her room. Gently, he placed her on her bed. His gaze dropped down her body and with great handiwork, he removed the T-shirt. Then he bent his head, kissed her lightly, skimming her mouth and face, before he moved down her neck and shoulders. He looked up at her, and the fire in his eyes told her how much he must have missed her.

"Tell me about your dreams," Mat murmured against her breasts.

"I'm dreaming it again. This time it feels real."

He chuckled and then flicked her nipple with his tongue. "Like this."

She gasped. Oh God, yes, like that, yet so much better. A moan escaped her lips when his mouth moved down along her body, finding all her sensitive spots again, teasing her, and exploring. Blood rushed through her, heating her skin wherever his mouth touched her. Her whole body was humming and heat pooled between her legs. When he found her most sensitive spot, she arched into him as he stroked and caressed until she gasped, giving in to the pleasure.

He moved up her body and lowered himself again. "Like music to my ears."

"Please, Mat."

"Tell me what you want, baby," he whispered, as he held her through her shudders.

"I want you. I need you."

He brushed his thumb across her lower lip with a tenderness that almost did her in, and she wrapped her legs around him as he slipped inside her. Slow at first, but gradually with deeper and stronger strokes. Her nails dug into his skin as she rocked into him when she came again, letting him sink in even deeper. With a gentleness she'd come to know of him, he tangled his hand in her short hair and tugged so their gazes met dead on.

****

Mat held her close, enjoying having Tiffany back in arms. Making love to her was different. It wasn't sex. It was an experience of exploring, searching, and being one. He couldn't get enough of it. Looking into her blue eyes when she'd come, he'd seen the depths of her soul, and it'd touched him. In more ways than one.

He trailed a finger down her cheek. "I've been dreaming about you, too," he whispered into her ear. "This was so much better, though."

Tiffany moved in his arms, and the simple change of having her breasts against his skin told him he hadn't had enough, yet.

She kissed him. "I'm sorry for the way I treated you. I truly am. But I needed some space."

"I understand."

With a gentle shake of her head, she continued. "I was overwhelmed by everything. There was too much going on at once. The past came back to haunt me. The future was so close but I was scared to hold onto it, because the past." She sighed. "But I should've never said no to you when you offered to come over."

She wriggled out of his arms and a sense of sudden loss of her body and her warmth evoked some strong emotions. After she'd returned to

Melbourne, he had carried the same emptiness inside him. He wanted to reach out for her to move her back into his arms, but watched as she reached for a big piece of paper before she held it up to show him.

"I'm a very stubborn person, unfortunately. I needed to get things done first. Deal with the guilt I felt and still feel inside, but most importantly I had to close the chapter on Hudson. I'm beyond relieved this is over. So I came up with a to-do-list."

He glanced at it. It was helping her father get better, finish some assignments, learn about helicopters, plan a tour through New Zealand, and the last item of her list, framed by hearts on both sides, was *Call Mat and tell him how much he means to me.*

"I've never been good at waiting," he said.

She laughed. "So I see. I'm so glad you're here."

"Me, too."

She dropped the piece of paper to the floor and moved back into his arms. He pulled her closer, kissed her, ready for the next round.

After a shower together later that day, they sat on the couch enjoying the pizza they'd ordered. She told him about the attack and how scared she'd been despite knowing the police had an unmarked car just around the corner. Leaving the house each day not knowing whether that day was the day had pulled on her nerves. Her relief was obvious. Tiffany also told him about her father and his recovery. They planned to visit him the next day.

She looked at him. "How long will you be staying?"

"If you'll have me, a few days."

Her smile told him she was enjoying the moment as much as he was. Even with Steve's hint about coming over to Melbourne, he'd been so nervous about the trip. He'd been anxious like never before. Flying a group of tourists through a sudden change of bad weather had seemed like a breeze compared to coming to see her. And even though he was aware they'd only talked a little during their lovemaking session that morning, they'd been honest words.

So he knew he was ready.

He stood, walked out the front door to his car, and retrieved a little box he'd picked up the previous day.

The smile she gave him, when he returned, made his heart skip a beat. It gave him the assurance he was about to do the right thing.

He sat next to her and took her hand. "Tiffany?"

A small frown appeared on her face, and he pinched the bridge of his nose, hoping he wasn't about to muck this up. He smiled as he smoothed her frown with his thumb.

"I love you," he whispered as he met her gaze. Studying her face carefully, he waited for any reaction, whether it'd be another frown, a smile, a laugh, or even tears. Her expression, however, didn't change much, but she stared at him with her mouth open. So he carried on. "I know this is a big leap, for you as well as for me, but I believe it's the right one." He flicked open the box to reveal the three-stone-ring, with the diamonds in a woven design, before finally asking, "Will you marry me?"

She still stared at him, with her mouth open, before her gazed drifted to the ring. Carefully, she touched it. A silence hung heavy between them.

"I…I…I'm…"

Her unspoken words were like a stab into his heart, and after a long moment, he drew in a deep breath, determined not to give up.

"I know we haven't known each other long and it'd be a leap of faith—"

"Mat, I'd be leaping a few thousand kilometres, a leap from one country to another."

"Who says you'd need to move to New Zealand?"

Eyes wide, she stared at him again.

"If it meant I'll be with you, I'd come to Melbourne."

"You need the mountains, Mat. You need the fresh air. You need Lucy—"

"I need you," he said softly.

Again, she touched the ring, and he would have given anything to read her thoughts.

"I was so scared when I came back to Melbourne. Seeing Dad in hospital, and it was all my fault." She sighed, but he knew she hadn't finished, yet. "I was scared of losing you, and all the while I almost lost my mind. Being back in Melbourne felt wrong." Her hand moved from the ring to his face as she cupped his cheek.

Seeing the tears in her eyes, Mat was scared as well. Scared of losing her.

When she stood, his instinct told him to grab her hand and pull her back to him, but he didn't, knowing she needed room to breathe. She walked over to her little desk before returning with a framed picture of them at the edge of Lake Wakatipu.

"I don't think I've ever felt so at peace with the world and myself like I did when I was with you in New Zealand."

A rush of relief howled through him, although it wasn't the answer he'd hoped for.

She moved closer to him and took his hand. "Aren't you worried I could be—"

"A bitch? And ugly? And gay?"

She laughed. "Yes."

"No, I'm not. I know you're the sexiest, but also the kindest and most thoughtful woman I've ever been with. You're intelligent, determined, and witty. And you're the woman I want to spend the rest of my life with."

She kissed him, and he returned it, putting everything into it — his waiting, his desire, and all of his love he had for her.

When she broke the kiss, she smiled. "Give me time..." She stopped and bit her lip before explaining. "That came out wrong." The side of her mouth pulled up in a grin. "Wrong choice of words. Sorry." Hastily giving him another kiss, she moved onto his lap. "It was a *yes*. That's what I wanted to say. *Yes. Yes. Yes.* As long as you don't expect me to move tomorrow."

He narrowed his eyes. "A yes with conditions?"

She snorted. "Oh, my God. I'm ruining the whole wonderful situation here."

"Baby, ko nui taku aroha koe.[9]"

---

[9] Words can't express how much I love you.

"That is what you said at the airport."

"It means words can't express how much I love you." His mouth curled up in a smile. "I already knew then how much I loved you." With his hands trembling, he took the ring out of the box and placed it on her finger. "Will you marry me, taku whaiāipo[10]?"

"Yes, I will."

He slid his hand into her hair and brought her face so close to his their noses touched. "I love you."

"I love you, too," she replied softly. "And I couldn't think of anything better than to spend the rest of my life with you."

---

[10] My sweetheart.

Thank you for reading "Their Bond through Jade"

♥

FOR NEWS ON UPCOMING books, sign up for Iris' Newsletter and receive a free book as well. Or join her FB Group. If you enjoyed the journey to Hobart in Tasmania, please consider following Iris on Bookbub so you won't miss any upcoming releases.

If you liked Tiffany and Mat's story you might like to read IN THE SHADOWS OF A LIE as well. Lani lost her mother in an accident and she's now determined to meet the man who, according to her mother's diaries, is her father. He's not what she expected, a bit on the extravagant side, but she soon warms up to him, thanks no less to Dylan, her father's neighbour. Despite her attraction to Dylan, she can't figure out whether he's a friend or foe.

Questions or comments? Find Iris on the following social networks:
Website: http://www.irisblobel.com/
Newsletter: http://eepurl.com/bQ68rL
Twitter: http://www.twitter.com/_iris_b
Bookbub: https://www.bookbub.com/authors/iris-blobel

Printed in Great Britain
by Amazon